THE DRAGON PRINCE'S BRIDE

ELVA BIRCH

Copyright © 2021 by Elva Birch

All rights reserved.

No part of this book may be reproduced in any form or by any electronic or mechanical means, including information storage and retrieval systems, without written permission from the author, except for the use of brief quotations in a book review.

ROYAL DRAGONS OF ALASKA

This book is part of the Royal Dragons of Alaska series. All of my work stands alone (always a satisfying happy ever after and no cliffhangers!) but there is a story arc across books. This is the order the series may be most enjoyed:

The Dragon Prince of Alaska (Book 1)
The Dragon Prince's Librarian (Book 2)
The Dragon Prince's Bride (Book 3)
The Dragon Prince's Secret (Book 4)
The Dragon Prince's Magic (Book 5)

Subscribe to Elva Birch's mailing list and join her in her Reader's Retreat at Facebook for sneak previews and sales!

1

"Yes, Mother," Leinani said.

She wasn't actually sure what she was replying to; all of her attention was outside the window, at the snowy landscape flying by outside their car. But 'Yes, Mother,' was a safe reply to just about anything.

Leinani wished they were going slower. There was so much to see, and it made her dizzy to watch the strange trees dash by.

And, to be honest, she was in no hurry to arrive at their destination; these were her last moments of *freedom*.

It was so surreal, to be in an arranged marriage, in this day and age. Leinani hadn't really expected to marry for love, but she'd thought that maybe she wouldn't have to marry at all.

As the oldest child of Mo'orea royalty, she had been groomed to rule, and then breathed a sigh of relief when the oldest of her brothers found his mate and was cemented as heir. She didn't mind being spared the weight of the responsibility, but it left her feeling adrift and directionless.

She didn't envy her brother his happiness, but she sometimes felt wistfully that it would be nice to have a destiny.

And now, somehow, she did.

Mo'orea's ally, Alaska, needed a queen for their eldest son in order to clarify their succession, so here she was, thousands of miles north of her home, rushing to bind herself to a complete stranger with a magical spell.

She would trade her tropical island home for a palace in the snow, giving up surfing for skiing. It would be an adventure, she told herself. There was a hollow spot inside of her that wanted a purpose, and here it was before her.

Prince Fask had been kind, in their correspondence, and their conversations on the phone had been reassuring. He was polite, had a sense of humor, and was handsome. She could have done a lot worse.

She was going to marry Fask and be Queen of Alaska at his side. If it wasn't a fate that she had ever imagined, it certainly wasn't a future to dread.

Her mother said something else she didn't catch, and Leinani again said, "Yes, Mother," and hoped it would suffice.

Angel Hot Springs Resort opened out of the forest around them, a busy little cluster of grand buildings milling with people. Guards at the front gate waved them through.

Leinani took a deep breath and soothed her fluttering nerves.

Soon, her dragon murmured.

There would be a lengthy ceremony for Toren and Carina's marriage. Then, a quiet, private activation of the mate bond according to the Compact, the magical contract that dictated the relations of all the Small Kingdoms. Then...

She scratched a little hole in the frost gathering on the window as the car slowly approached the largest building, with its impressively tall double doors. She could probably enter it in her dragon form.

Here, her dragon said, rising suddenly within her. *We are supposed to be here,* **now.**

It was so undeniable, utterly irresistible. Leinani felt a wave of relief crash over her. It felt like everything was happening exactly as it should, and she was, for the first time, completely *comfortable* with what lay ahead. She was going to meet her mate, and they would marry, and she would be a queen, just as she was meant to be.

She slipped from the car as soon as it rolled to a stop, smiling at the uniformed guard who took her hand to help her out. The guard was a Native woman with chin tattoos and golden star buttons who didn't smile back.

It didn't dampen Leinani's relief in the slightest, and she moved forward confidently, not even waiting for her parents behind her. The air was bitingly cold, but the bitter temperature didn't bother her; it was something else entirely that had Leniani stepping forward as swiftly as she could for the waiting hall.

There, her dragon breathed in her head, leading her unerringly up the steps. Guards saluted and opened one of the double doors at her approach.

It was warm inside, and icy mist swirled with her into the bright-lit lobby.

Had they already performed the ceremony? That wasn't the plan, and she hadn't thought that was even possible without her participation, but the draw was absolutely unmistakable. She shrugged out of her coat and let them lift it from her, then marched, not through the double doors into the hall where guests were gathering in anticipation of the start of the wedding itself, but to a smaller door through an alcove on the left.

No one thought to stop her.

Leinani didn't pause, didn't hesitate even a moment. She turned to a narrow stairway tucked behind a corner, gathered her tapa cloth skirt into her hands, and was halfway up the flight when a figure appeared at the top, hurrying towards her with the exact same urgency.

They stopped just a step apart, and Leinani, already at a disadvantage due to her shorter stature, had to crane her head awkwardly back to smile up at...*him*.

It was her husband-to-be.

She was confident that he would make her happier than she'd ever had any reason to hope she could be, and Leinani couldn't *wait* to make him her own.

There was winter sunlight streaming in through a window to their right, and his dark hair glowed in gold, his face shadowed as he stared down at her.

Leinani felt giddy, awash with eagerness and delight. Her dragon felt incandescent in her chest, happy, confident, and slightly smug, the way she often was.

Then he very suddenly sat down, so hard that the stairs trembled, and they were gazing at each other, face to face.

Leinani's heart dropped from her chest and dismay quenched every ounce of her desire.

This was unmistakably her mate, but it wasn't *Fask* at all.

2

Tray sat because his knees wouldn't hold him any longer.

He knew who she was, of course: Leinani, crown princess of their ally, Mo'orea, oldest daughter of the king and queen. And she was here to marry his brother.

No... his dragon hissed in his ear. *She is ours.*

The sense of something coming had been like bees in his ears for days now. Even before the royal family left Fairbanks to come to Angel Hot Springs for Toren and Carina's big wedding to-do, even before his twin brother Rian and Tania had announced their own engagement, Tray had known that he was supposed to be somewhere, do something...meet someone.

He hadn't wanted to mention it to anyone, not sure enough to make a declaration and risk his brothers' teasing. He'd watched what Rian had gone through before he finally flew to Florida to scoop up his librarian mate, and he'd watched the fireworks before that when their baby brother Toren declared that his mate was a woman who was wanted for murder.

It was already absurd that there were two mates. The Compact that bound Alaska to the Small Kingdom Alliance was supposed to decide the next king by selecting him a mate. The magical document ensured that they met, and that they knew each other when the time was right. Now, here was Alaska with not one, but two mated heirs already, and neither one of them wanted to be king.

Three, if Tray counted himself. Which he didn't. He couldn't!

Fask was the one who ought to be king. Everyone agreed on that point. Not just because he was the eldest; he was the solid, responsible one. The statesman. The one who enjoyed politicking, who knew how to talk people around to things, and felt most at home in council rooms and courts. So when Tania and Rian sleuthed out a loophole in the Compact that would allow them to bind Fask to the oldest child of their ally, it seemed like the perfect solution.

Marrying Fask to Leinani solved the confusion of succession, imported a queen who had actually been trained to lead, and allowed Tania and Carina to breathe a sigh of relief, as neither one of them had the slightest interest in ruling.

It was logical. It was elegant. It was...

"Impossible!" Leinani was clinging to the stair railing like she was afraid that her own legs would give out.

She was more beautiful than any of her photographs, with waves of dark hair with just a hint of red framing a round, golden-brown face. Her eyes were glittering and golden, wide with shock, and her lips—perfectly painted and full—were slightly parted. She wasn't as short and delicate as Tray had imagined she would be, with strong bare arms that showed distinct muscle in soft curves. She was wearing a sleeveless dress that seemed to be embroidered paper, cream and brown. It looked like it would crinkle if Tray were to draw her into his arms where she belonged.

"You're Leinani," Tray said, after they had stared at each other for an unmarked time. He probably ought to add something to that, he thought. Princess, or Your Highness.

"And you are Prince Grantraykist."

His full name, on those amazing lips, made Tray shiver.

"This—" he started, just as she said, "I'm—"

Ours, his dragon hissed.

"You go first," Tray said quickly.

She drew in a slow, steadying breath. "This is rather awkward," she said with serenity that Tray didn't believe for a moment. He could feel her in his mind, feel the same confusion and yearning that was eating up his own concentration. She wasn't experiencing any less confusion or intensity than he was, she was only better at *pretending* she wasn't.

She dragged her gaze away and smoothed down the skirt of her long dress. "I'm here to marry your brother."

Tray clenched his fists in his lap. Sitting a step above where she was standing, he was looking slightly up at her. "You're my—"

"Mate," they said together, and Tray heard the hitch to her breath.

"Clearly, there's been some kind of mistake," Leinani said softly.

Tray laughed humorlessly. "It was a *mistake* when Rian found a mate after Toren did. This is more than a mistake. I'm beginning to think that the Compact has gone completely off the rails."

Neither of them denied that they were mates; what was the point? It was exactly as Rian and Toren had described.

Tray felt the same curious, deep connection, the immediate recognition. It wasn't just lust and longing; he knew that this woman was the absolute key to all of his potential happiness. She was a heady mix of familiar and utterly unexpected, and he wanted her in ways he hadn't even known were possible.

When she chuckled at Tray's observation, his heart expanded seven times and he vowed to make her do it again at every opportunity. No sound in the world had ever been so rewarding. "What do we do?" he asked, because crushing her into his arms and kissing her dizzy simply wasn't an option.

She licked her lips and reluctantly said, "Nothing."

"You're..."

"I'm here to marry your brother. We'll do the ceremony, and...this will be sorted. I'm supposed to be *his* mate."

"You think that ridiculous pledge of the twenty-first section will...fix this?" It was hard to think of it as something to fix. His dragon was firmly convinced that it was right and correct, not just a terrible mistake.

Leinani cocked her head, somehow managing to look more adorable and also very smart as she considered. "I don't see why it wouldn't. The language of the Compact is very specific. It's set up kind of like a computer program, and this is an if, then statement. *If* we meet the criteria, and *if* we say the right words, *then* a mate can be chosen." She paused, brow furrowing. "Except..."

"Encumbered. This could definitely count as an encumbrance."

"You're familiar with the passages in question."

Was she surprised? Tray knew he had the reputation of being a feckless jock, especially when held up against his scholarly twin brother Rian, and he found that the idea she might assume he was the idiot the media made him out to be actually stung.

"It's been a major topic of discussion lately at the dinner table," Tray said defensively. It wasn't like him to care what people thought, but he did now. With her. "So, if the ceremony doesn't work, what then?" Then she would be his, he thought, and the hope that shot through him was at least partly hers.

He almost kissed her, then, on the strength of the possibility, but she was better at reining herself back in and she quickly said, "Then we wait. Spells fade."

"Is that really all that this is? A spell?" Tray asked quietly. It seemed impossible that everything he was feeling —that they were feeling—could possibly be magic. It felt too deep, too true.

Her eyes glittered. "It's a future possibility," she whispered. "What we...*might* feel for each other, given the right conditions."

"Our future *possibility*." Tray had never wanted a future so badly; he'd never imagined this kind of connection, never envisioned someone as amazing as Leinani.

"If we don't enable this possible future, it won't happen. After a few weeks, the...encumbrance...will be gone and I can pledge to your brother free and clear."

Tray looked away and made a wordless sound of frustration and anger. He had never hated Fask as much as he did in that moment. He was as certain as his dragon was that this, *this* was what was supposed to be. Leinani was his, and his only.

"I know," she whispered, and Tray dared to look up at her face again. Her stoic expression had slipped into misery. As if she realized it at the same time he did, she tipped her chin up and blinked, and Tray watched in fascination as she pursed her lips and forced her face back into composure. He had never seen anything so brave, and he could feel the effort it took to achieve. She brushed down her skirt again, a gesture that he could sense gave her a tiny amount of comfort. "I shouldn't keep them waiting."

"Screw them," Tray said ferociously. "What about you? What do you *want*?"

She didn't answer, and didn't have to. She wanted him as desperately as he wanted her, as deeply. And she was better than he was, because she was strong enough to turn away, back down the stairs and leave him behind, step by agonizing step.

3

Walking away from Tray, her dragon raging in the hollow cavity of her chest, was the hardest thing Leinani had ever done in her life. If she had not found her mother at the bottom of the stairs, she might have turned around to hurl herself back up to him. As it was, she could not quite keep from glancing back, to find that the prince had vanished.

His last question hung in her head. What *did* she want? She'd come to Alaska to shoehorn herself into destiny, and destiny had taken her by the hand and offered her an even better possibility.

But if she followed her heart, she betrayed her promise and disrupted *two* families. She couldn't be so selfish.

"Lei! Darling, where did you go in such a hurry? We want you to meet you Prince Fask, we'll all be sitting together for the ceremony. The wedding ceremony, that is! Your ceremony will come after, of course, and you'll be center stage. Hemi! Oh, Hemi, I've found her!"

Lienani's father was standing at the entrance to the great hall with a man that Leinani knew at once from the photographs she had studied. They were flanked by guards and a photographer with a press tag was taking photos into the crowd. He turned to shoot in her direction.

Smile, Leinani told herself, but a blank expression was all that she had to offer the man she was here to marry. She let her mother draw her forward, and politely offered her hand.

"Princess Leinani," Fask said warmly, taking her hand in a firm, possessive grip.

It was everything she could do not to jerk it away from him.

Fask was handsome, she supposed, trying to be fair. He was tall, and dark-haired, like Tray. He had a short, tidy beard and she worked very hard to convince herself that it was only because she disliked facial hair that Tray seemed any more beautiful. They had similar chiseled features, and the same silvery-blue eyes.

But they weren't Tray's eyes, and it wasn't Tray's brow, and it wasn't his jaw beneath the beard, and it wasn't his mouth… "Your Highness," she finally remembered to say, and she used a curtsy as an excuse to extract her hand.

"May I offer you an escort into the hall?" Fask asked.

He looked surprised and pleased, Leinani thought bitterly. Like she'd met some standard that he hadn't expected her to reach. For a moment, she felt sorry for him, because he was never going to be able to measure up to the man she'd just met. "Thank you, Your Highness." She put her hand into the fold of his elbow and tried again to smile at him.

Her dragon gave a chorus of complaint in her head, which didn't help her attempt in the slightest.

"Don't they look lovely?" Leinani's mother said in a stage whisper behind them. "Hemi, do you remember when that was us? Our little girl!"

Leinani's father made a gruff noise and she wondered if he didn't guess a little of her consternation; he never said much, preferring to let his wife carry conversations, but he had always been aware of the moods around him.

"This is Drayger, a, ah, dragon of Majorca," Fask introduced, when a deeply-tanned man met them at the entrance and offered Leinani's hand a kiss.

"Ever the statesman," Drayger laughed. He hadn't let go of Leinani's hand. "I am the illegitimate son of the king of Majorca. One of several, I might add. We're hard to keep track of."

He had been one of the many guests that Leinani had familiarized herself with before coming. "It is a pleasure to meet you," she said, able to think of little but the pain in Tray's face, pain that had been a mirror of her own. She took her hand back, and Fask was quick to lead her away, as if he was worried that Drayger might charm her away from him.

It might have been funny if Leinani hadn't already been hopelessly mired in a storm of desire for his brother.

They mingled with guests and visiting royalty for an agonizing time before the wedding itself, making small talk and observations about the weather and the decor. It wasn't a large event, as these things went, and the guest list was very tightly curated. Leinani knew most of them by reputation and photograph, if not personally: Alaska's immediate allies. The most important dignitaries. A smattering of close celebrity friends. A smiling, sobbing woman who wore a badge that proclaimed she was president of the Toren Facebook Fan Club.

Leinani remained on Fask's arm as they toured the event hall, and he and her mother hinted unsubtly to everyone they spoke to that they should be sure to linger after the wedding for a second, special announcement, looking pointedly at Leinani. She still hadn't managed to smile, but she kept her expression dutifully neutral.

"How lovely to meet you," she fibbed to a bored-looking royal from the Siberian Islands while Fask talked politics with the dragon King and Queen of Japan. "What a beautiful place for a wedding!"

"It's frightfully cold," the prince complained. "They could have picked a warmer place to do this."

Not a dragon shifter then; the cold didn't bother Leinani any more than the heat of her home island did. "I understand that the hot springs are quite comfortable," she offered conversationally. "Have you enjoyed them, yet?"

She honestly longed to swim. Her favorite escape was the bay by their castle, where she could swim out in either of her forms, long strokes taking her further and further from land.

Even just imagining how it felt to float in the salt water made her feel a little better. Just her, and the sea and the sky, everything else lost in the distant surf...

Her thoughts drifted like the current until she was imagining Tray in the water with her, his silver eyes laughing, his voice...his hands....

A bell chimed through her daydream and the prince's answer. Leinani realized she was smiling foolishly at nothing...and Fask was gazing down at her.

"Toren and Carina are finally ready," he said, when she had schooled her face. "I have you seated next to me."

The random milling of the guests began to take direction and everyone flowed to their seats with a buzz of anticipation.

Fask led Leinani to the very front of the room, wearing her on his arm like a badge, and Leinani was aware of the speculative looks and the eyes glancing speculatively at the engraved silver rings on her fingers. She sat gracefully in the chair next to him, her mother sliding in beside her on the other side. Beyond Fask, his brothers trickled in, along with a young woman with an ornate cane carrying flowers.

Leinani felt Tray's entrance, all the hairs on the back of her neck rising with the sudden draw of his presence. He was late, nearly everyone was seated, and someone called a joking greeting to him, "Nice of you to show up."

Someone else asked in a stage whisper, "What have you done this time?"

Leinani heard the prince take a seat at the far end of the aisle and desperately wanted to lean forward so she could crane around Fask and see him again.

But she knew too well that if she saw him, all the feelings she was very unsuccessfully trying to keep in check would be utterly overwhelming, and she'd lose whatever claim she had on calm.

"Are you alright?" Fask asked quietly. He had taken her hand at some point without her notice and she realized that she was clutching at his hand unconsciously.

"Yes," she said, dropping it with more force than she intended. "Of course, I'm sorry."

He gave her an indulgent smile, patting her hand gently, and Leinani was saved by the sound of a wedding march starting.

She spent the wedding staring through the ceremony, toying with her rings, horribly aware that Tray was only a few people away from her. She sat ramrod straight in her chair, not letting herself lean forward or ease back, for fear that she might accidentally catch a glimpse of him out of the corner of her eye.

Her mother hadn't missed Leinani's clasp of Fask's hand, and tried in vain to catch her attention several times.

It wasn't a long wedding, as state events went; clearly the American bride had insisted on keeping it simple, with an abridged version of the recitation of ancestors and a brief exchange of vows. Their kiss at the end was informal and passionate, and the audience applauded as they descended from the dais to a rain of rose petals and a swell of music.

Leinani stood with the royal family, and let Fask lead her to the banquet hall, grateful that Tray disappeared swiftly before them. Even knowing he was in the same huge room made her knees feel weak.

"I thought we would do our ceremony quietly to the side now," Fask said, talking to her parents as much as to her, "and then announce the happy news at the reception."

Everyone stared at her and Leinani had just enough self-possession to nod agreeably. "Of course," she said faintly, trying not to feel sick.

Fask led them to a small chamber off to the side where the rest of his family met them and Leinani did a dizzying round of handshakes and introductions. Raval was the grumpy-looking blond. Toren was the groom, and Carina his bubbly bride. Rian looked alarming like Tray, but didn't unsettle her nearly as much, and Tania, the woman at his side, was wearing a large, glittering engagement ring. Kenth, the second-oldest, appeared to be missing, as well as Tray.

Leinani greeted them all on diplomatic autopilot, congratulating Toren and Carina, admiring Tania's beautiful cane without drawing undue attention to the fact that she needed it. She introduced her parents and her brother, praised the food, and commented on the beautiful Alaska scenery, all of it practiced and completely without second thought.

Her mother clung to her arm, squeezing her in excitement, and after they had done all their diligent niceties, there was an expectant silence.

"Let's get started," Fask said smoothly, and he put his hand out to Leinani.

Her mother let go of her arm and gave her a gentle push. They automatically divided the room, Mo'orea behind Leinani, Alaska behind Fask, and Leinani made her feet close the distance between them.

Fask took both of her hands in his and glanced at Tania and Rian. "All we have to do is say, 'I pledge of the twenty-first section,'" he confirmed.

"Hopefully," Rian said with a one-shoulder shrug. "It hasn't been tested."

"Hard to do a trial run on that one," Tania added shyly.

Fask turned back to Leinani and she forced herself to look up into his face, just as the door to the private room burst open.

"Better late than never," Raval grumbled.

Leinani was looking at Fask and she stared at him as hard as she could so that she wouldn't turn to glance at Tray. Was he going to make a crazy last-minute stand for her? He wouldn't be so foolish, would he?

Part of her longed for him to do it, and she was not honestly sure she wouldn't drop Fask's hands and throw herself at Tray if he made the slightest protest.

"Sorry," he growled, and even just that made Leinani want to pull her hands from Fask and go to him. She heard him edge around her parents and go to the other side of the room, as far away from her as he could get.

Fask shot his brother an amused look and then his attention was back on Leinani. "As I was saying, I pledge of the twenty-first section."

Leinani opened her mouth, and then shut it again. Her mother made a tiny noise of poorly-suppressed excitement.

She didn't want this. Her dragon didn't want this.

Every fiber of her being wanted Tray, every tiny thought was focused completely on him.

It's just a spell, she reminded herself. It's just a mistake, and she would set a second spell that would overcome the first and everything would play out exactly as it should. She would feel this crazy for Fask until they learned to genuinely love each other and everyone would be happy, most of all herself.

Her dragon howled in her head, completely unconvinced, but Leinani shut her out with all her will and blurted, "I pledge of the twenty-first section."

And nothing happened.

She was still a knot of longing and desire for the wrong brother and Fask was looking at her dubiously.

After a moment of tense silence, he asked, "Is it supposed to happen right away?"

No one could answer him, of course.

"There's nothing specific about the timeline," Tania said with quiet authority.

"The implication is that it would be immediate," Rian said.

"Implications can be misleading," Tania reminded him. "We have the first fruit, the choice…"

"You don't have any older children I don't know about do you, Hemi?" Leinani's mother teased, clearly trying to lighten the mood.

"I promise I do not, my darling," he answered patiently, to some chuckles.

"Are either of them encumbered?" Tania asked thoughtfully.

Fask was still looking at Leinani, and she was staring back at him because if she didn't, she would look somewhere more dangerous.

"No," he said firmly, eyebrows knit in confusion.

"Yes," whispered Leinani, and the entire room stilled and stared at her.

"What do you mean, sweetheart?" her mother finally asked. "What on earth are you talking about?"

"Lei?" her father prodded.

Fask's hands on hers only tightened.

"When I got here," Leinani said, closing her eyes. "I was called to find my mate. I had hoped...that this would take precedence."

She decided she didn't enjoy making rooms go quiet with shock and when she opened her eyes, she frowned across at Fask.

She gave a tiny tug on her hands, hoping to take them back discreetly. He didn't let go and she didn't want to make it a thing, so she stood quietly, waiting.

"Why would the Compact do that?" Raval wanted to know.

"Idiotic document," Rian complained.

"This is absurd!" Leinani's mother exclaimed. "How could it happen?"

Carina snorted in shocked laughter and Toren smothered a chuckle.

There was a hand at her shoulder, squeezing tight in support. Her father. Leinani looked up in gratitude.

"Who is it?" Fask asked then, and there was another awful lull in the conversation, everyone focused on her.

Leinani didn't dare look, didn't dare point, couldn't speak.

And then Tray laughed.

"Who would you least want it to be?" he asked mockingly, and he moved out from behind the others.

4

The only upside to having everyone in the room turn and stare at him in appalled shock, was that they finally stopped staring at Leinani, who didn't deserve their prickly appraisal and judgy looks.

Tray gave an exaggerated shrug, happy to take the spotlight from her if it was the least he could do. "Hey, I didn't ask for this! C'mon, like I would want that kind of responsibility."

It wasn't worse than taking a puck to the chest, he thought.

"We already spoke," Leinani said, with her quiet authority. "We'll just weather out the mate spell and try the ceremony again once it has faded." She looked at Tania with a sudden stab of uncertainty that hit Tray somewhere behind his breastbone. "It goes away, right?"

"It does fade," Tania assured her. "A couple of weeks, maybe?" She gave a slow, shy smile at Rian. "Long enough for him to win my heart."

"Long enough to make peace with the idea of a

crown," Carina said, adjusting her sparkling tiara. "Oh, crud, there goes another hairpin."

"The Compact can't make you fall in love," Rian said, looking at Tray with unexpected pity that did nothing to make Tray feel better. "It just gives you...a kind of an echo from the future. A *possible* future. Nothing says we can't change that."

"We'll just stay apart from each other," Tray said, as carelessly as he could manage. He spoke to Leinani, because she was the only one in the room that mattered to him at the moment. "This will fade like a bad dream, and once the encumbrance is gone, you can pledge of the twenty-first whatever and get married and this will be the kind of thing we laugh about over Christmas dinner two years from now. 'Remember that time the Compact accidentally picked Tray? Whew! Boy, did we dodge a bullet!'"

"Yes," Leinani's mother said gratefully, giving Tray a smile. "That will work beautifully. Nothing needs to change at all."

There was a feeling of relief in the room. It was a neat solution, everyone was happy with it. Everyone except Tray...and Leinani. He could feel her conflicted emotions, so entwined with his own. He'd never wanted anything more than he wanted her, and she ached with longing in return.

They were looking at her expectantly and Tray was awed by the way that she could stuff down all her own desires to calmly say, "Yes, of course. That's the perfect plan," exactly as if she was accepting a cup of tea.

"The press is waiting in the reception room," Toren reminded them. "They're expecting some kind of big announcement. What are you going to tell them?"

"We could announce Tania and Rian's engagement,"

Carina suggested. She grinned at Tania, who made a face and shook her head.

"That's not news," Raval scoffed. "Everyone's known about that for ages."

"Since before we were *actually* engaged," Rian chuckled.

"We should stick to the original announcement," Fask said, in his most obnoxious I've-made-up-my-mind voice. "When the compulsion fades, in a few weeks, we'll perform the ceremony and the end result will be exactly the same."

Tray had to look away, because calling what he felt for Leinani a compulsion felt like a betrayal, and the idea of Fask marrying Leinani made him want to punch a hole in something. When he could look back, Fask was holding a ring out to Leinani.

He wasn't sure what was worse, watching him slip it onto her finger, or feeling the wave of despair and wrongness from her. Only reminding himself that what he felt were false future feelings kept him from shifting and tearing the building apart with his claws. This was the smart thing to do, the logical thing. He'd be glad for this choice. Maybe he and Leinani could even be friends, eventually, and he'd have nothing but sisterly feelings for her.

Leinani's mother gave a muffled squeal of excitement and hugged Leinani around her unprotesting shoulders. There was an awkward scattering of congratulations.

"This actually seems fitting," Carina laughed kindly, as she moved forward to embrace Leinani. "Everyone thought Tania and Rian were engaged long before they actually were, and we were engaged before Toren ever got around to asking me. Why shouldn't you have an engagement before a mate, just to mix things up a little!"

"This family does engagements very oddly," Tania

agreed. She gave Leinani an awkward sideways hug, hindered by her cane.

Rian offered a hand and Leinani shook it gravely.

Raval was next. "Welcome to the family," he said wryly. "Good luck with us."

It would have been Tray's turn next, but he didn't dare shake her hand. Touching her, feeling her skin against his...it would have undone all of the self-control he'd managed, and he knew that it would undo hers as well. He'd have to kiss her, have to claim her for his own. He moved back to the far edge of the room, and let everyone else leave to announce the happy news.

The room went quiet with everyone gone, though Tray could still hear the applause that came with the announcement and see the camera flashes through the open door.

"Tray?"

As identical twins, he and Rian had always been close. On the surface, they couldn't be more different; Tray liked sports, Rian liked books, and they clashed goodnaturedly on most topics. They didn't agree on movies or music, girls or drinks. Rian talked about getting a cat, Tray was solidly a guy who liked dogs. And for all of that, Tray knew that Rian would always have his back, more than any of his other brothers, in the most irritating way possible.

So it wasn't entirely unexpected that Rian opened his arms and folded Tray into a quick, heartfelt embrace.

"I'm sorry, Tray," Rian said, shaking his head. "I can't imagine if someone had told me I had to let Tania go right after we met."

"Imagine if she was marrying Fask," Tray said miserably.

"Fask...our brother is a good man," Rian said dubiously. "He'll make a good king."

"And a *great* husband," Tray snarled. "He's all loyalty and lordliness. That doesn't make it any better."

"It will be," Rian promised. "It *will* be better."

Knowing that Rian was trying to help didn't make Tray feel any less prickly. "For you, maybe. You aren't watching your mate go marry another man."

"It shouldn't hurt for long," Rian said stoically, like he was talking about a broken arm or a strained wing.

"How long?" Tray wanted to know. "How long do I have to feel like this? How many hours of this godawful turmoil do I have to put up with?"

But even Rian, the analytical one, didn't have an answer for that. "I didn't notice when it faded," he admitted. "I was busy falling in love with her for real and it all sort of blurred together. I figured out how to read and understand her so well that I never exactly missed when it wasn't being fed into my head anymore. I think it was a couple of weeks before I realized that I didn't still have that lodestar pull in my chest. And what was left...it was every bit as much magic."

What would Tray have left at the end? Would his heart burn out altogether? He was absolutely certain he'd never have anything else in his life like Leinani. Even if he could make peace with her finding happiness without him, he would be utterly ruined for any other love. There was no one else in the world for him.

"I'm leaving," he said. "I'll go back to Fairbanks early, it will be best if I'm not underfoot."

"Stay for the family game?" Rian suggested. "They're making me play, and it's always been a highlight of a visit here, for you."

Tray stuffed back his panic. "I can't see her again, Rian. I can't be around her, I can't see her pretend this isn't a thing. I can barely pretend it isn't a thing in a room by myself."

"She won't want to come to a midnight hockey game," Rian scoffed. "Fask wouldn't be so cruel as to make her. It will just be us, and you can skate off some steam before you go. Drayger is playing Kenth's position, so it wouldn't be even without you."

Tray shook his head. "No, I can't. I won't. I just want to get out of here."

"I get it," Rian said sympathetically. "Maybe go for a soak in the hot pools while everyone else is busy with wedding and engag—uh...things. Miss the rush, then steal dinner from the kitchen like I did when we were kids and I wanted to skip out on something formal and boring."

"You always pinned your raids on me," Tray chuckled.

"All I had to do was wear a hockey jersey and no one even questioned it," Rian said with a grin. "See, you look more human already. Go drown your sorrows and try to avoid drowning yourself. Maybe Angel will show up and give you some sage advice." Officially, the hot springs were named after an outcropping of rocks that looked a little like a praying angel on a nearby ridge. In reality, Angel was a water spirit who watched over the pools. She allowed visitors in the cooler pools, but was jealous about the use of the hotter, higher pools, frequently glamoring them invisible.

The spirit had taken an interest in the royal family, and had, to everyone's surprise, gone out of her way to introduce herself to Tania and Carina. She had been inscrutable when asked about the fact that there were multiple mates, confusing the line of succession, but then, Tray had always found her mysterious.

"The last time I asked Angel for advice about a girl,

she recommended adding hot pepper powder to Fask's hand lotion."

Rian laughed. "That was Angel's idea? Angel, the cranky water spirit who never gives a straight answer to anything?"

"I'd been planning on just adding it to his food."

"Pedestrian," Rian observed.

Outside the doorway, there were more cheers and applause and Tray felt a sickening drop to his stomach. Would she kiss Fask for the cameras?

Ours, his dragon rumbled in quiet rage.

Rian said something, but Tray was fighting his dragon too hard to hear him. Maybe a dragon-strength hockey game really was exactly what he needed to burn their frustration away.

5

Leinani had hoped it would be easier to walk away from Tray the second time, and it wasn't at all.

It didn't matter that this parting had an audience, or that they had just very logically explained why they were distancing themselves. It didn't matter that she was wearing another man's ring. Every fiber of her being wanted to step into Tray's arms and stay there forever. Forcing herself to go out into the wedding reception on Fask's elbow to try smiling at the cameras and announce their engagement was seven kinds of terrible.

She heard the announcement itself like she was listening to it over a tinny radio, or down a long hallway, standing next to Fask before the members of the press and the visiting royalty. He managed to look happy enough for both of them, and Leinani hoped she looked mysterious and distant, not just heartbroken.

This will pass, she told herself. This is only temporary. In a few weeks, this will be an amusing moment in my history.

Then there was a pregnant pause and Leinani realized

that everyone was waiting to see if Fask was going to kiss her.

He didn't, perhaps knowing she wouldn't welcome it, and she felt a rush of gratitude. He was kind, and he was handsome, and that was really all she'd hoped for. They could build from this, when her heart was her own again.

The press wanted to ask questions, and Leinani was glad that Fask deflected them for her. Her attempt to smile at him went a little better after that, and when the room was cleared for dancing, she was happy to accept.

She could dance in her sleep, and to be honest, she felt exactly like a sleepwalker. She turned slowly around the room like a wind-up jewelry box dancer, first with Fask and then with a series of royalty and diplomats who wanted to congratulate her.

She did a decent job at conversations, she thought, all things considered. "It is an excellent match," everyone said. "You look so good together," a few added.

"I am sure we will be very happy," she lied, over and over again. She hoped, but she wasn't *sure* at all.

By the time she could politely beg off, she was disappointed to find that neither Carina nor Tania was still there. She'd nursed a faint hope that they might have words of wisdom regarding what she was going through and they had seemed genuinely kind and welcoming.

But Carina and Toren had disappeared early in the dancing, to everyone's knowing amusement, and Tania and Rian had begged off not long after. Raval trotted Leinani dutifully around the floor without saying much and then returned her to Fask with a sigh of relief.

"I'm sorry this didn't go more smoothly," she told Fask. Distance from Tray was definitely helping her calm; she felt like she could think again, and when she smiled, she thought it at least felt marginally more successful. "I certainly didn't mean to be this much trouble, Your Highness."

Fask, who had been politely leading her off the dance floor, stopped dead in his tracks. "Princess, please take no blame. In no way could this be considered your fault." He frowned at her, then he raised her hand to his mouth and kissed it. "It will heighten the anticipation, waiting for the spell to fade."

It took every shred of her self-control not to snatch her hand back and shrink away. The terrible wrong feeling of it was unmistakable, like a sour note played too loud in a quiet symphony. But it wasn't Fask's fault any more than it was her fault, or Tray's, and Leinani reminded herself that she was only being subjected to outside forces, that her instincts were faulty. She just had to get through this, like she was surfing a curl that felt out of control; she just had to ride it to the shore.

"Thank you, Your Highness," she murmured, taking her hand back as soon as she could without making a fuss. "Everyone has been very kind."

"Fask," he said. "Of course you must simply call me Fask. Some of the family will be gathering in the hot pools for a soak, would you care to join us?"

Family—did that mean *Tray*? No, he wouldn't be there, not if she was being invited. Leinani missed the opportunity to return Fask's offer of familiarity in her wave of panic. "I am feeling fatigued," she confessed quietly. "It has been an...exciting day as an understatement, and I should like to retire now."

For an awful moment, she thought Fask was going to offer to walk her to her rooms...and possibly request the kiss in private that he didn't press for in public. But she should have trusted him, and was relieved when he kindly said, "Yes, of course. We have arranged a set of rooms for you in the West Hall. I will have someone show you the way. Ah, your majesties, I was just saying good night to the princess."

While her father nodded solemnly at Fask, her mother swept Leinani into a spontaneous embrace. "Darling, you must be exhausted. You have been an inspiration. We are so proud of you."

Leinani wasn't sure how much she'd actually done, wandering around the party in a haze of confusion and misery, juggling her own feelings, Tray's, and all their future—*possible* future—emotions, the new ring on her finger like a sparkling lead weight. She hugged her mother back, careful for both of their tapa cloth dresses and jewels. "I'm looking forward to a shower and a good night's sleep," she agreed.

"Here's Captain Luke to show you the way to your rooms," Fask said, introducing the Native woman who had opened the door for Leinani what felt like a lifetime ago just that afternoon. She was carrying their coats. "If you need any food, or anything at all, please don't hesitate to ask."

"Thank you," Leinani said, unable to even think about food.

Fask kissed her hand one last time and then she was free at last to put on her coat, pulling the fur up over her ears, and follow the captain out of the event building to the nearby lodge, flanked by guards.

She and her parents each had a generous suite of rooms, richly and tastefully appointed. Leinani was distantly glad that dead animals didn't play as large a role in the decor as she'd feared; Alaska still had a reputation as a frontier and when she had first imagined living here, she had dreaded being asked to hunt and use an outhouse in the snow. The lengthy drive from Fairbanks to Angel Hot Springs had done little to dispel that image.

Fortunately, it appeared that there was copious hot water and coffee makers and computers and all the trappings of civilization, even here, a ridiculously long drive through the wilderness from the capital city.

Leinani made all the polite noises of appreciation and pushed her parents off with hugs, told the maid she would unpack herself, then finally shut her door and was alone, for the first time since she'd arrived and had her life turned upside down.

She wearily considered unpacking, but went instead to the window, pushing aside heavy curtains to look only at her own reflection in the dark glass, unsmiling and slightly smudged. It took her a moment to realize that it was because there were multiple panes of glass, each of them with a faint reflection, so that she looked blurred.

She *felt* blurred. Blurred and stretched into pieces, duty warring with false magical instincts.

She let the thick curtains fall back over the window, kicked off her shoes, and sank back into the bed, only to jerk back to her feet at the sound of a knock on her door.

It wasn't Tray, was all that she could think at first, with a stab of disappointment. It was ridiculous that she wanted it to be, of course, and she trudged to open the door, wiping away tears she hadn't realized that she had shed as she schooled her features and put her shoes back on.

Carina was standing with Tania, holding a bottle of wine. "Oh, Leinani, we wanted to see if you wanted to come watch the midnight game with us. It starts in about an hour."

"Game?" Leinani wracked her brain, trying to remember if she'd been told about a game in one of the conversations she'd floated through. She automatically stood aside and gestured invitingly to the sitting area. "What game?"

"Hockey," Carina said with relish, trotting in and throwing herself down on one of the plush chairs. "A private midnight game where they don't have to hide their shifter strength and speed. It's apparently a family tradition after formal events like this."

Tania added cautiously, "Rian said that Tray wouldn't be there."

Even the sound of his name was like a twist in the gut, but Leinani was grateful for the information.

Carina plowed on merrily, "I imagine that it's a relief to have a chance to use their natural talents."

Tania looked a little shy as she took a much more careful seat than Carina, and hesitantly added, "I understand that you're a dragon shifter, too?"

Leinani sat carefully in the remaining chair as Carina got back up as energetically as she'd sat and went to the bar to find a corkscrew and glasses. "I am," she said serenely. She could see the curiosity that Tania was trying to hide behind her manners and offered, "You're welcome to ask any questions you have." These women would be her sisters and she knew that having allies in the castle would be valuable.

"Oo," Carina said. "Do you get cold? I know that Toren can handle a lot larger a range of hot and cold than I can, but it was twenty below today and you're from the tropics. Didn't that bother you?"

"I wasn't outside very long," Leinani said, accepting the glass of wine that Carina offered. "I could feel that it was cold, but I don't think it was as uncomfortable for me as you find it."

"None for me," Tania said regretfully to Carina's lift of

an empty glass of wine. "New medication, and I don't want to skew the data."

"Oh, that's lovely," Carina said, without a trace of the embarrassment that Leinani was feeling about the reference to Tania's apparent frail health. "I hope it helps you."

"I'm cautiously optimistic," Tania said, with a curious set to her jaw that might have been stubbornness. "I've already made it through a pretty exciting day and actually feel like I still have enough energy for a late night superpowered hockey game. I might not be up for much tomorrow, though; I honestly can't tell if I'm just running on fumes or not. But I don't have to do anything tomorrow, so I can crash if I need to." She smiled rather foolishly down at the ring on her finger. "It would mean a lot to Rian if I was there."

Leinani caught herself playing with her newest ring absently, and made herself stop. "Let us know if you need to return early, of course," she said politely. "I don't know how long I will find it interesting to watch men hit a puck into a net with a stick."

"There's more to it than that," Carina protested, and she launched into an explanation of convoluted rules and techniques that Leinani could barely follow.

None of them mentioned Fask or Tray after that, and Leinani was grateful for the respite. She didn't think she'd have been able to sleep anyway, and she was happy for any distraction from her aching heart and grumbling dragon.

6

For a few blissful moments, Tray thought that Rian had been right, and a swift game of hockey really would burn off the worst of his discontent and despair.

The night was crisp and clear, once they were out of the perpetual fog that surrounded the hot pools, and it was a small personal party: just his brothers, Drayger, and Captain Luke, acting as referee. It wasn't a game for an audience, it was *family*, and they could be exactly as their natures suggested. Skating across the ice on the big rink was almost like flying, and it was a challenge against others of like skill and speed, facing Toren at center ice, dodging Drayger to pass the puck to Fask. It was three against three; Rian played goalie for his team, Raval for the other.

For a while, focusing on the stick in his hand and the puck on the ice, he could forget that anything had changed. They were just brothers, Drayger stepping into Kenth's role with an eerily similar grin. They were just playing a game, showing off their skills and testing their own limits. It was a game that required concentration, and that was just what Tray needed. He was relieved to find that centering on the play and the puck was something he could do.

Toren scored first, and circled the ice with his stick up in triumph as Rian laughed and shrugged, fishing the puck from the net to send it back towards Luke. She leaned down easily and scooped it up for the drop; she wasn't a dragon, but as a polar bear shifter, her strength and grace was nearly as great as theirs, and she could get out of their way swiftly when they came barreling down the ice at her.

The play went back and forth, the puck pinging off the sticks and backboards, singing through the air between them, intercepted, returned. Luke blew the whistle on icing, per their modified rules, and dropped the puck again. Drayger stole it, Rian blocked his attempt at the goal, but Toren swooped in for the rebound, just as Tray felt a sudden moment of panicked distraction.

Ours, his dragon insisted, swiveling his attention from the sport.

He knew she was coming well before the three women appeared at the edge of the ice, bundled warm in respect for human sensitivity to the bitter cold. Tania, Carina...and Leinani.

She had changed her embroidered paper ballgown for tailored gray pants. A fur-trimmed parka hood hid her beautiful face.

Carina climbed up on the boards, cheering enthusiastically for her new husband as he took advantage of the activity to make a second score on the rebound. Tania, more sedate and careful, only waved shyly to Rian, who missed blocking the shot from Toren. Luke whistled the score.

Tray had eyes only for Leinani, until he could force

himself to turn away, using his momentum to curve away, catching Fask's gaze instead.

Fask had a half-smile at his mouth, a knowing little look as he saw Tray trying not to stare.

For one blazing instant, Tray hated his brother, actually detested him to the bottom of his soul. Tray had never wanted Fask's responsibility, or his easy manners and casual charisma, or even a drop of the political power he wielded. But he wanted Leinani, the way he had never wanted a thing in his life. It was like his lungs wanting air.

The analogy made him realize that he'd been holding his breath, and he circled back around to where Luke was holding the puck, just beating Fask to the circle.

The captain gave him a sharp look, then shook her head and waved him back, her whistle in her teeth.

Tray realized that he was baring his teeth at her and skated ungracefully back to let Fask take the drop. Was it because Tray was too obviously worked up, or did Captain Luke want to give Fask a chance to show off in front of his bride-to-be?

Ours, his dragon steamed. ***Ours.***

But she wasn't his, she wasn't theirs, she was Fask's, and this was just *temporary*.

Tray actually missed the puck drop, working so hard to keep his dragon reined back, and he had to scramble on his skates to catch up with Fask, who had won the puck from Toren.

Fury gave him an extra burst of speed, and he caught up with Fask at the far end of the ice, slamming him into the boards.

"Aren't we on the same team?" Fask protested, half-laughing, but Tray was blind with rage, and when Fask lowered his stick, he dropped his own and balled fists in his gloves.

Luke's whistle penetrated his angry stupor, and Tray landed the punch on the boards instead of his brother, splintering a hole into the perimeter of the rink. Toren and Drayger glided by in slow arcs, clearly prepared to haul him off of Fask if it came to that, but staying out of arm's length.

Rage slowly faded to awareness and Tray drew a shaky breath, expelling it in a cloud of steam. "Sorry," he said, not at all apologetic.

The pity in Fask's face was worst of all. "I get it," he said mildly. "She's really something."

She was more than just something. And as hard as Tray tried to convince himself that it was all just a temporary inconvenience, he knew that there was nothing in the world as wrong as Leinani marrying anyone but him.

"You don't get it," he snarled back. "You don't get it at all. You have no idea."

He still wanted desperately to pound Fask into a smear on the ice, and he reminded himself that it wasn't Fask's fault. It wasn't his fault. It wasn't her fault. No one was at fault, and nothing was going to bring him satisfaction...maybe ever.

"It's okay," Fask was saying magnanimously. "Give it some time, find a new girl…"

Tray didn't want his useless advice or his politician platitudes, and the idea that he could ever find anyone like Leinani raised the hair at the back of his neck. He bristled, raising both fists in a wave of rage. Fask looked genuinely afraid and cowered back for one brief, satisfying moment before Tray could wrestle himself back. He pushed back violently and before Toren and Drayger could close the distance, he was shifting and leaping up from the ice with a sweep of wings that knocked everyone back from him.

"Let him go!" he heard Fask say as the ground fell away below him.

Only then did he realize that Leinani was already gone, streaking as a dragon up into the sky above.

His dragon had complete control, dragging him in helpless pursuit as he struggled to regain his wits.

7

At first, it was simply headlong flight up into the sky, going only away, anywhere *away*.

Leinani strained her wings, flying harder, faster, darting up into the cold air and dark sky, holding her breath until she thought her chest might burst. Up and up she rose, above the clouds, where she finally slowed her ascent and gazed around, hovering on slow-beating wings.

Above the clouds, she might have been anywhere in the world, the last rays of sunlight just past the horizon barely staining the puffy, solid-looking sea. Only the white peaks of distant mountains that broke them looked any different than her home might look from this height on a cloudy day. She banked, not south in chase of her beloved sun, but north, slowly now, sucking thin air into lungs that wanted to scream instead.

She struggled with her dragon, who wordlessly wanted to return to their mate.

It's a mistake, she told her fiercely. *Tray is not our mate. We are here to be Fask's bride.*

But her dragon didn't care for promises or for Fask at all. She wanted Tray, only Tray...and Leinani could not fault her.

The clouds thinned and the foreign land below became slowly visible in the light of the nearly full moon. The hues from the sunset lingered impossibly long as Leinani continued her flight; she was used to a sun that plunged swiftly into the sea, not one that wandered in a shallow glide down to flirt with the horizon and shyly hide, casting color into the sky for hours after it had technically set.

The mountains glowed in stark, pastel shadows, all craggy peaks and glacier-covered glory, and pale snow-blanketed forests spread out for impossible distances between them. Leinani had never seen a land so vast and...in its own inhospitable way, so beautiful.

It wasn't long before she became aware that she wasn't alone in the sky.

The other dragon was giving her plenty of space, the edge-of-the-eye glimmer of them staying respectfully back, pacing her, but not pressuring her.

She knew at once that it was Tray, both by her dragon's kittenish delight, and by his distance. Any of the other brothers would have been sent to escort her back, or at least to protect her and offer her an honor guard, and they would be at an ascribed distance, not trailing so far behind. This dragon followed as if he could do nothing else, as if he was drawn to her as she was to him. Her head was a hopeless tangle of what she felt and what he felt and she didn't recognize that she was drifting towards him until they had looped through several huge circles in the darkening sky.

He gave a bobble of his wings and veered away at last, Leinani trailing him with the same careful distance as he'd given her. He led her to a rocky outcropping on an alpine peak, wind-scrubbed of snow, and dropped onto it, perching elegantly and arching his long, dark neck.

Leinani landed neatly at the other edge of the precipice, and what had been barely enough space between two dragons with outstretched wings was a ridiculous distance between two humans when they both shifted.

"You shouldn't be here," she cried, while all of the rest of her seemed to scream that he should. She had to repeat it, louder, and she sighed and closed the space between them when he still couldn't hear. He was incredibly tall, she thought, until she noticed that he was wearing his hockey skates still.

"I shouldn't be here," Tray said, as soon as they were close enough. "What did you say?"

"That you shouldn't be here," Leilani said, smiling despite herself. She felt the craziest things about him. Not just lust and longing, though that was certainly there too. Worse were the stupid, irrational feelings, like *safe* and *trusting*. Like he was her closest friend, her confidante.

They found exactly the distance that allowed them to speak without exceeding their ability to resist the temptation to reach out and touch one another and Leilani huddled into her parka. She wasn't cold, exactly, but it cradled her the way she wished that Tray would. "I'm not running away," she promised. "That's not what this is. I only needed…"

"…to fly," Tray finished. "I know. I *know*."

It was too dark to make out his features well. The moon was behind him and he was edged all in silver, the color leached away with the slow departure of the sun. She could feel the grief from him, the same frustration and despair that was swelling in her own chest.

They were quiet for a time, the only sound the muttering of the wind all around them. It snatched at the little furballs hanging from her hood and dragged fingers through Leinani's hair.

"I only came to tell you..." Tray finally started.

Leinani waited until she realized that he might not be capable of continuing. "You're leaving," she finished for him. Just saying it made her dragon seize in agony and she fought to keep her face serene, even though Tray probably couldn't make out her features in the deepening dark. It was pointless; he could feel everything she was, anyway.

"I'm leaving," Tray agreed mournfully. "I can't stay here, I can't. There isn't a castle big enough. *Alaska* isn't big enough. I don't know if the whole world is big enough, but I have to go try."

"It will get better," Leinani said, trying to convince herself. "The spell will fade, we'll be just as we were before. It's just...something that could have been." Something amazing. Something that would have completed her. She felt tears welling in her eyes and willed them back.

Tray made a noise of frustration and anger that might have frightened her if he had been anyone else, if she hadn't been able to feel how much he hurt. It was almost impossible to pick his pain from her own.

"This is what we have to do," Leinani said, keeping her voice firm. "And I can't go, so you must. I am sorry to chase you from your home. It isn't fair..."

"It *isn't* fair," Tray snarled.

"But this is how it is," Leinani said, voice rising despite herself. "And we are grown, responsible royals who can make choices that are smart and foresightful and best for our people." She was speaking as much to her dragon as she was to him. "Even if we don't want to."

She hadn't meant to add the last bit, it was as if it was

torn from her, and she bit her lip to keep from confessing more.

"Leinani…"

Her name in his voice threatened to break her. "You have to go," she said.

"I know…"

They stood without words, the wind howling at them as they wrestled back their instincts and their dragons.

Would her mate bond with Fask, fabricated through a loophole in the Compact, ever hold a candle to the real thing? Could she outlast this impulse and find any happiness with Tray's brother that compared?

No, her dragon wailed. *This one! Only this one!*

We don't get to choose! Leinani cried in return.

Then Tray was turning aside, and for a moment, all the planes of his handsome face were etched in moonlight before he was striding for the edge of the cliff and falling over.

She ran two steps after him before she could stop herself at the edge of the rocky outcropping, and watched the barest glimmer of his dragon form spiral below.

At first, she thought it was just her tears and the shimmer of his natural cloaking that made him look as though he was writhing. Then all his surprise and panic and pain struck her like a hammer. Lightning began to crackle all around him as his glide turned into a downward tumble, and without stopping to think, she shifted and flung herself down after him, her wings back in a furious dive.

Tray cried out in warning, but before Leinani could reach him, she passed through a weird, cold wave in the air and every nerve ending seemed to light on fire. Her wings unfolded, fluttering as her dive turned into a crazy freefall.

Abruptly, the air all around them went bright and thick

and hot and Leinani felt like her skeleton was being pulled out of her dragonhide.

Her last thought before blackness took her was optimism that maybe one kind of pain could burn out the other.

8

Tray came awake like he was swimming up in a bowl of gelatin. His eyes felt like they'd been sewn shut and every muscle in his body ached.

He'd fallen, he remembered, and the memory of Leinani diving after him made him struggle against the metaphorical stitches in his eyelids. A spell. Some kind of magic that had pulled at him, jerked him away from one place to...where?

He wasn't quite capable of sitting up; the attempt only made his battered body twitch ungracefully. When he opened his eyes, he found that he was stretched out on a cheap carpeted floor, and he blinked several times to focus. It wasn't a large room, and Leinani was lying stone still just an arm's length away, still dressed in her winter parka.

The sight of her drove strength into his limbs and Tray dragged himself closer. "Leinani," he whispered with a dry tongue. "Leinani..." He dared to touch her arm with one hand. "Princess?"

She stirred minutely but didn't wake, and Tray was

slowly aware of other people in the room, and the room itself.

It was a generic hotel room, all in cheap oatmeal colors, with windows above a long couch showing black squares of night. They were in a tiny sitting area with an uncomfortable-looking chair, a low coffee table tipped up on its side to make room for Tray and Leinani on the floor.

The air felt wrong, too warm and tacky for the dry winter climate they'd left behind; Tray guessed at once that they weren't in Alaska any longer.

There were two young men in nondescript khaki camouflage, watching them from a safe distance across the room, just past a king-sized bed. Both had rifles trained on them. A surge of anger made Tray's mind feel clearer.

Tray reached for his dragon, fully prepared to shift and make these two regret all their life decisions and maybe their parents' life decisions, too. He just had to protect Leinani from any collateral damage and...

Something was off. His dragon was there, coming back from the sluggish half-drugged place like Tray himself, but there was something blocking their ability to change forms. When he tried, it was like he was choking, like something was in the way of his airway.

Tray touched this throat and his fingers found a coarse string around his neck, hung with some kind of beads. The instant he touched it, he was enveloped in agony.

It was a spell, he guessed, something separate from the magic that had caught them, knocked them unconscious, and brought them to this place. When he reached up to it again and tried to tear the necklace away from his throat, it was as if his entire body was suddenly lit on fire, pain echoing down every nerve.

Hissing, Tray let his hand drop away.

The two men smirked and looked less alarmed, the tips of their guns drooping. One of the rifles looked ordinary, the other was covered with strange engravings. "I wouldn't try that again, Your Highness," one of them scoffed in an Eastern European accent. "That little trinket should keep any dragon from shifting or removing it."

Tray tried again, perversely, and only succeeded in biting his own tongue and spasming uselessly. Maybe if he was more recovered from the spell that had captured him?

He could sit now, though he wouldn't have trusted his ability to stand even if he hadn't been wearing skates. Leinani was just starting to stir.

"What did you do to her?" he demanded. "What did you do to me? Who are you?"

"Look," the other one said, "She says we ain't going to hurt you." He had an American accent, with a distinct whine to it.

"No," the scoffing European corrected him, "she said we won't hurt them *yet*. She didn't think she'd catch this one so soon so the rest isn't ready."

Then Leinani made a low, miserable noise and moved her arm. Tray ignored the guards and crawled back to her. "Leinani," he said, low and anxious.

Her eyes opened as sluggishly as his had, and she blinked at him in confusion. "Tray," she said in relief. A tiny smile appeared and vanished twice as fast. "What is happening? Where are we? What's wrong with me?"

Tray could not quite resist touching her cheek and knew at once that it was a dreadful mistake. He pulled his hand back swiftly. "I don't know," he admitted. "We've been captured."

Leinani blinked at him. "Ransom?" she guessed. He could almost watch her gather her thoughts and focus.

"You can ask these fine gentlemen," Tray suggested. He wanted to help her sit up, particularly after watching her flail and find her limbs unresponsive, but didn't dare. If the guards thought it was weird that he didn't offer his hand, they didn't say as much.

With effort, Leinani propped herself up against the couch and gave the guards a brave, steely gaze. "Do you know who we are, or what kind of trouble you are about to be in?"

She gathered herself, drawing in a deep breath, and then let it out in confusion as she reached for her own throat.

"Don't touch it!" Tray warned too late and her fingers found a necklace at her throat. Where his collar was coarse thread and rough beads, she was wearing an engraved choker, and when she tried to put her fingers beneath it, she arched in pain that burned away the last of Tray's fatigue.

"Leinani!" He surged forward on his knees, catching her as she slipped sideways and propping her back up as quickly as he could. "Are you okay?"

"I'm at least more awake now," she said through gritted teeth. There was a streak of blood at her lip and Tray had to make himself let go of her and not try to wipe it away.

"See, that one works, too," the guard that Tray was picturing as Scoff said with satisfaction. He didn't look intimidated anymore, only slightly smug.

"What about the spell on the room?" the whiner asked anxiously.

"All part of the same thing," Scoff said confidently. "The dragons can't leave this room without activating their restraints unless one of us says they can. Almighty dragons, brought low by pieces of string and bits of leather."

The other guard looked unconvinced.

Tray made the mistake of brushing fingers against the string necklace again and couldn't quite keep himself from hissing in pain. Worse, Leinani did, too, because of the mate bond.

"This is the kind of magic we'll all have," the first guard said confidently. "We'll have unlimited power at our fingertips. That's what Amara is going to give us, wait and see, my brother."

"Amara?" Tray blurted. "A tall, dark-haired woman, recently missing a few fingers?"

That earned him sharp looks from both of the guards, and Leinani.

"You talk too much," the whiney American said sharply. "C'mon, we should get Amara up. She'll want to see them right away."

Scoff shrugged, and they both backed cautiously away. Tray started to stand, which was when he remembered that he was still wearing hockey skates.

The guards realized it at the same time. "We'll take those with us," Scoff said.

"Do we have to?" Whiny asked.

"He's got knives strapped to his feet. We're not leaving them with him." Scoff's gun was raised to train on Tray, light glinting off of the etched barrel.

The fear that rose in his throat wasn't his own, but it wasn't any less keen for being Leinani's terror for him.

"Hold your horses," Tray said, bending to unlace them. "I expect these back at the end of my stay. They have sentimental value!" He loosened the laces and pulled them off, one at a time, then handed them over. One of his socks had a hole at the toe that had been chewed by an enthusiastic puppy.

They took the skates carefully and backed away down the tiny corridor between the closet and the bathroom door to the door to the room. Then they were out the door, latching it firmly behind them. Tray listened for the sound of an extra lock or bolt, but it never came.

He suspected that it would have been unnecessary anyway.

9

Leinani was finally starting to feel human, and when Tray helped her sit up on the couch, she had to be careful not to cling to him. "Thank you," she said shyly. They settled at almost opposite ends of the couch. Leinani shrugged out of her overcoat, kicked off her fur-lined boots, and looked around curiously.

"My cellphone is gone," Tray observed.

Leinani patted her pocket. "Mine, too. I imagine the guards took them while we were out. But I still have my rings!" She clutched, not at Fask's diamond engagement ring, but at the two silver rings on her other hand. Tray gave her a quizzical look, but didn't ask and Leinani wasn't ready to volunteer any information. Her earrings were still there, too, little gold hibiscus flowers with emeralds in the middle. "They weren't after valuables."

The hotel room was small and pedestrian; the bed wasn't even in a separate room from the little sitting area. There were pale rectangles on the wall where a television and missing pieces of artwork had hung, and there was a tiny kitchenette with a microwave, a dorm-sized fridge, and a coffee maker. The floor was cheap, knobby carpet, and the color scheme was almost uncomfortably beige. Windows along the wall behind the couch were so dark that they acted as mirrors.

There was no way to tell where they were, it was all as generic as could be, but Leinani was pretty sure they were no longer in Alaska. The electrical outlets were round, with round holes.

"Man," Tray said, just a little too jovially, "I've had some impressive hangovers, but this one does beat them all."

"Who is Amara?" Leinani asked, not sure if she wanted to know the answer.

"We're not really sure," Tray said. "But three times she has tried to steal our pages of the Compact. On her second to the last visit, she left some fingers behind when a portal closed unexpectedly."

Leinani hissed. Each of the Small Kingdoms had a copy of the Compact, as well as a few pages of the original. It was generally agreed to be one of most powerful magical items in existence, and fiercely protected. "How does she even know about the Compact?" Most people outside of Small Kingdoms royalty and extremely trusted circles only knew about the public version, greatly sanitized and presented as a curiously archaic but completely mundane legal document, with no references to dragons. But then, most people didn't know about magic, either, and these people clearly did.

Tray frowned. "We know she has some connections with a cult that's gained some prominence recently, some kind of magical equality movement. We caught one of her goons the last time she made a try for the pages, but he wasn't very useful, just babbled a lot of rhetoric about balance and reward. I'd bet money that these guys have the same tattoos, a black axe set in a kind of a labyrinth."

Leinani touched the choker at her neck and whimpered at the wave of pain that swept over her.

"Stop doing that," Tray begged her, clearly aborting his own movement to reach out to her. He made fists and put his hands at his sides.

"It's like an itch," Leinani said apologetically. "Or a hangnail. So why would she capture us? Does she intend to ransom us for pages of the Compact? What would she even do with them?"

"Tania suggested that the Compact could be altered."

"Altered? Why? How? Wait, is that why there were two mates called for Alaska?"

Tray spread his hands helplessly. "No one has any idea. And that's three mates, now, thank you very much."

Leinani blinked at the reminder. Tray was her mate. *Three* princes had been tapped in succession.

Mistaken mate, she cautioned her eager dragon. *This is all just a misunderstanding of some kind. A paperwork problem, apparently.*

It was easier to think about being kidnapped than it was to pine over Tray. "They can't honestly think that they can get away with this, can they? Neither one of our families is going to take kindly to our abduction." She felt stronger already, anger burning away some of the confusion in her mind and the weakness in her limbs. "They're probably already searching for us. It will only be a matter of time before these people feel the full impact of our kingdoms' wrath and come to regret what they've done."

Tray made a little noise that Leinani wouldn't have been able to identify if she couldn't feel his hesitation.

"You don't agree?" Leinani pursued.

"They probably think we ran away," Tray pointed out. "To be...*together*."

Leinani let her breath out with a little wave of helplessness. Together. To be with Tray, as his. To have him for herself... It took all her concentration to rip herself away from the idea, and the dismay that followed dampened her ardor. He was right. Both families knew that she and Tray were entangled in the mate spell, they probably just assumed that neither of them had been strong enough to resist it, choosing instead to flee their responsibilities and answer their own needs. She was equal parts frustrated that they would think she was so weak and dismayed to think that it was quite likely that no one was searching for them.

She was on her own. No, she was on her own with *Tray*, the one person she really, really needed not to be alone with.

"Very well," she said, as calmly as she could. "We can't plan on any rescue coming. We either escape on our own, or wait patiently while they finish...whatever it is they are finishing...and contact our families to negotiate for whatever it is that they want."

She felt strong and clear-headed enough now to stand up, so she did, prowling around the room and resisting the urge to play with her collar. "What do you know about the spell that is supposed to keep us here? Could we break out of a window and jump down? Do we even know what's down there?" It was too dark to see anything but reflections in the window, and Tray's was distracting. She wandered to the nearest wall and put her fingers on it. There was a warning buzz at her throat. She could just touch the plaster, but she knew that trying to break through it would come with consequences.

Tray stood with her, and shrugged. "They didn't

exactly give me an orientation brochure," he said. "I'm the brawn here, not the brain."

Behind his bluster, Leinani had a glimpse of the same uncertainty she'd felt before. He was sensitive about feeling stupid, particularly, she guessed, when he was held up next to his scholarly twin brother. She had to squash her impulse to reach out and comfort him and looked down, instead.

There was a hole in the toe of his left sock. Leinani wanted to feel that this was a sign of how completely inappropriate he was for her, but instead she found it weirdly charming and down to earth.

They quietly explored the room, opening drawers and looking under the bed. It had clearly been stripped—there was no clock radio, no television, no telephone. There wasn't even a pen and pad of paper, a Bible, or a room service menu. Leinani's stomach rumbled, and she wished she hadn't been too distraught to eat dinner, however many hours ago that had been.

Tray tried the door handle and staggered back from it in agony that had Leinani screwing her eyes shut and trying not to scream. When she opened them again, Tray was fighting his way through the spell towards the door again.

"No, don't!"

When his hand closed on the handle, he jerked like he'd been struck by lightning and fell back from the door to lie still on the floor.

Leinani fell to her knees at his side. "Tray? Tray?"

Relief flooded through her as he cracked an eyelid to look at her. "Am I okay?" he asked plaintively.

"I told you not to do that," she said, keeping her voice steady even though she knew that he must have felt her panic.

"Sorry, your highness," Tray said, clearing his throat and sitting up.

The short corridor by the hotel door was narrow, and they were crowded close in the little space by the closet and the door to the small bathroom. Leinani was hyper aware of his broad shoulders and how easy it would be to fall into his arms, and how much she craved that comfort. It was more dangerous than sex, she realized. The moment she let herself seek solace in his embrace was the moment she would lose her heart; it wasn't passion that was most dangerous, it was compassion. And she didn't dare do that, so instead she backed up carefully and stood. "Don't try that again."

"Duly noted," Tray said, climbing back to his own feet.

Then the door handle gave a rattle and just as Leinani wondered if she would be able to withstand the spell long enough to lock it and keep the guards out, the handle swiveled and the door opened. They probably had a master key anyway.

This was Amara, Leinani guessed at once, with her guards standing worshipfully behind her, their heads bowed.

She was the kind of woman that was generally called handsome, with strong, symmetrical features. Her hair was loose around her, long and dark. She held her hands before her, and Leinani's quick, curious glance showed that one of her hands was bandaged, though if she was actually missing fingers, it wasn't obvious.

Tray and Leinani, without consulting each other, held their ground, not inviting her in and not allowing her the space to pass them without actually pushing them aside. It was a common diplomatic tactic, not giving up any space not declared, and Leinani spared a moment to wonder how much diplomatic training Tray actually had.

"What the hell is this all about?" he demanded.

Not much, apparently.

Leinani drew herself up, giving Amara a steely look. "I wish to discuss the terms of our release," she said, as firmly and reasonably as she could manage. It didn't volunteer any information and set an initial position of power, whether she actually had any or not.

Amara looked amused by both of them. "You are Princess Leinani of Mo'orea, Flower of the Island and a firstborn dragon. You are recently engaged to Prince Fask of Alaska. Quite recently, actually."

Leinani wasn't terribly surprised. Amara clearly knew the dragon secret of the Small Kingdoms royalty, and Leinani's engagement photos had probably been on the Internet within hours. It wouldn't take much sleuthing to discover her identity once it had been narrowed to 'dragon' and her distinctive Island looks.

"I'm sure that my fiancé will greatly appreciate our safe return," Leinani said gently, curving her mouth into a smile more successful than any she had offered at Carina and Toren's wedding.

Amara gave her a tolerant smirk in return.

Tray didn't even attempt politeness. "And by appreciate, her highness means that you are about to face a fuckton of angry dragons."

Amara's smile only broadened. "You are Prince Tray of Alaska, fourth son of the dragon king of Alaska, twin of Rian. I find it terribly interesting that neither of your families has raised any kind of alert about your absence yet. Almost as curious as catching the two of you in one net." She looked between them thoughtfully, pursing her lips. "Almost as if you had run off together...for some reason."

Leinani was surprised by the leap of logic. There was, of course, no way that she could know that Leinani and

Tray had been mistakenly bound; only their immediate families knew that, and none of them would say anything about it.

"How did you know where to set your trap?" Tray wanted to know, and Leinani could feel his sudden swell of guilt.

"We've been watching for some time, waiting to make our move. My spies identified places that you liked to visit. I understand that's a place you often go cliff-diving with your brothers."

Tray's guilt made Leinani want to apologize, even though she wasn't sure why he felt so bad. Then she remembered that he had led her to the cliff where they'd spoken together. He clearly thought it was his entirely fault that they'd been captured. But if she hadn't fled from the hockey game, neither of them would have been there at all.

"That's irrelevant," Leinani said smoothly, hoping to fight them both out of the feedback loop of self-blame. "What is that you want in exchange for us?" Would she ask for *both* of their family's pages of the Compact? Leinani didn't want to make suggestions that would betray what little they knew.

"In exchange for you?" Amara said, and her smile split into a merry laugh. "I don't want anything *for* you, I want something *from* you. You will remain my guests for the time. To be frank, I was not expecting our gambit to pay off for some time; I am a patient and persistent woman. We have more preparations to finish before you can step into your destiny."

Leinani's dragon had definite ideas about what *their* destiny was, and Leinani was sure it wasn't at all what Amara had in mind.

"What destiny?" Tray demanded.

Amara looked at him with a look so serene and confident that Leinani was a little afraid. It was the expression of a madman, someone sure of their path, terrifyingly certain of their own superiority, locked into a fate of their own making. The kind of person who didn't see people as people, but only as impediments or stepping stones.

Her focus made Leinani feel small and uncertain, and she dredged into her training to find her next step.

"Won't you come in," Leinani said graciously, stepping aside and gesturing Amara past the bed as if the grungy little hotel room was the finest conference room. "There is no reason at all to stand here in the hallway when we have business to discuss."

"How sensible of you, your highness," Amara said easily.

But Leinani already knew that sensible in this case wasn't going to save them.

10

*L*einani was a master politician, Tray realized at once.

She really was a perfect match for Fask, he thought mournfully, to his dragon's distress. He folded aside and let the princess lead Amara to the seating area where they'd only recently regained consciousness. The princess moved their coats and her boots, tidying the area like a housewife who'd been caught unprepared for a delightful guest as she made ridiculous smalltalk about the limited decor.

"I'm afraid I have no refreshment to offer," she said, gesturing Amara to the single chair. She frowned distastefully at the guns that the guards were holding as they followed her in hesitantly. "You may put those down. We have tested your defenses; it is clear that you have no need for those weapons. Go and put the coffee table down, then take these things to the closet." She gestured at the coffee table, which was still on one end, leaning against the wall.

The guards looked askance at Amara, who smiled tolerantly and nodded.

Tray had a moment of wondering if she was trying to coordinate an escape. Should he try to overpower the guards? Was she trying to signal some kind of plan through her tumultuous feelings? A telepathic bond would have been a whole lot more useful than this emotional mess. He eyed the guards, both of whom looked strong and fast. He was probably stronger and faster; he had a good chance with them if Leinani thought she could overpower Amara. Which only left the spell around the room and the collars that were choking their dragons.

Leinani caught his eye and gave a tiny shake to her head.

As the guards set the sitting area to rights according to her commands, Tray sat at the edge of the bed rather than trying to safely divide the couch with Leinani.

"You must let me know if there is anything you need," Amara said politely.

Leinani looked around the room as if she was considering the idea for the first time. "I must confess that I am rather hungry," she admitted, sounding rather theatrically wan. "And I would certainly be grateful for a change of clothing and a pair of shoes. For both of us. Tray, is there anything else you need?"

"Our cellphones?" Tray suggested honestly.

Amara laughed and the guards chuckled.

Leinani laughed as well, a musical chime of sound. "I don't even know if mine would work here," she observed. "Where did you say we were?"

Amara did not fall for the obvious bait. "I'll see that you are brought regular meals and look into some clothing. As I said, we were not expecting...your *company* so soon."

"We certainly do not mean to put you out," Leinani said humbly, her voice like syrup. "Please know that we will cooperate in any way that we can."

Tray thought he should probably back her up in some way, but only scowled at Amara and wished he could throw the coffee table at her.

"You aren't what I expected," Amara admitted.

Leinani managed to look completely innocent. "I'm not sure what you mean."

"As dragons, I expected you to be...tougher."

Tray nearly laughed. Did Amara really believe Leinani's demure facade? He could feel her simmering dragon and her own indomitable will. She was feminine, and her manners were pretty, but he knew, better than anyone, the steel at the center of her soul. He almost felt sorry for Amara.

Almost.

Leinani, her golden eyes wide, said sweetly, "I'm sure that you've gotten a great deal of misinformation. It's clear you have impressive resources," she gestured to her necklace without actually touching it, "but I think you underestimate what rich allies we could be. I'm sure that there's no reason for dramatics like kidnapping, and we'll all be quite happy to set this behind us."

Tray marveled at the fact that she managed to give Amara a slight insult, a touch of flattery and just a little threat, all in a few carefully-crafted sentences.

Amara smiled, and any hope that Tray had for Leinani simply sweet-talking them out of their troubles vanished.

"You seem to think I'm interested in your wealth, or your political power, and I assure you, I have no need of that. I have riches that you would have trouble imagining, and your laughable Small Kingdoms are no match for my worldwide network of devoted followers. No, I have no need for your cooperation. I will take what I need from you, and I will enjoy seeing you humbled."

Her eyes went flinty cold, though her smile remained.

"Too long, you have enjoyed your life of privilege and power, suffocating the true roots of mankind. We will reclaim our magic from you all and restore balance to the world. We are preparing for war."

"You'll have to explain this to me," Leinani invited, her voice neutral, even though Tray could feel the alarm from her. "What do you mean by that?"

Amara didn't take the bait, but stood instead. Leinani rose to her feet politely, but Tray stayed seated at the edge of the bed, wiggling his toe through the hole in his sock. "I will see that your needs are met. Make yourselves comfortable, your *highnesses*. I give thanks to the powers that you were both delivered to us. It makes experimentation much more useful to have two of you to test things on."

Then the guards were respectfully trailing out after her and the door was snicking closed behind them.

"I don't like the sound of that," Tray admitted. "I don't know what she's planning but *testing*? *Experimentation*? That evangelistic glow to her eyes? Did you see the way the guards *looked* at her? This wasn't the most reassuring meeting I've ever sat through and that woman is completely nuts."

Leinani sighed and ran fingers back through her hair. "I have to agree," she said, sounding as discouraged as she felt.

"You were pretty amazing, though," Tray hastened to assure her. "I mean, all that crook'd finger stuff and *gosh, ma'am, where did you say we were?* You'll be a hell of a queen." His *brother's* queen, he remembered, with a stab of regret. Not that he wanted to be a king anyway.

"Your sock has a hole in it," Leinani said, voice strangled, as she swam through the regret and longing they were both drowning in.

"Pretty sexy, isn't it?" Tray asked, wiggling his toe.

"One of the puppies chewed a hole in it as I was leaving for the hot springs." It had only been that morning, he realized, feeling suddenly exhausted. Or yesterday morning, or tomorrow, however time zones made that work.

"You have puppies?" Leinani said in surprise.

"Four of them, about six weeks old," Tray said, glad for a safe subject. "I bet you're a cat person. All uptight and independent, constantly grooming yourself."

He was grateful that Leinani knew he was teasing her, and she smiled and touched her ruffled hair self-consciously. "I've never had a pet," she said unexpectedly.

"We definitely have to remedy that!" Tray said at once. "It's kind of a thing we do in Alaska now: new crown princesses get puppies. There are two boys left to choose from, both of them champion sock-chewers."

Leinani giggled. "They sound cute."

Tray could have waxed on about how smart and cute they were for some time, but there was a knock on the door then, and it opened without waiting on an invitation.

"Formal dinner for their highnesses," the guard said mockingly, and two small packets were tossed into the hotel room onto the bed. He was gone as quickly as he'd appeared.

Leinani rose to her feet and got entirely too close to Tray to pick them up off the beige comforter. "Oh, they're cold!" she exclaimed. "What are they?"

"Those, princess, are frozen pizza pockets," Tray told her. "Because this place just wasn't classy enough already."

11

The microwave was making crackling, popping noises.

"Is it supposed to do that?" Leinani asked, eyeing it leerily. It sounded like it might combust at any moment.

"I hope so," Tray said cheerfully. "Otherwise, our gourmet dinner is going to be as disappointing as our dining room. I couldn't find any candles and the butler is being terrifically slow. Far cry from the top floor of the Ritz," he sighed.

"I'll lodge a complaint with the management," Lenani said weakly. She felt a little shocky, like all the crazy things that had happened to them were finally catching up with her.

Tray was doing that thing where he didn't quite look at her face, but focused on a spot by her collarbone. "There aren't any napkins, have a hand towel." He handed it to her from arm's length just as the microwave gave a cheery little ding.

The coffee table was too short to sit at comfortably from the couch, so Leinani settled cross-legged on the floor in front of it as Tray, cursing over burnt fingers, fetched their dinner and sat across from her.

"Well this looks terrible. I mean...ah...how *interesting*," Leinani said, as it was placed before her.

"Very diplomatic, princess," Tray mocked her.

The defrosted pastry pockets were both soggy and greasy, and while they were sufficiently hot, their texture was enormously off-putting. Leinani was starving, so she squashed down her standards and took a large, brave bite. The flavor was not a great improvement on its appearance.

"They're considerably better from an oven," Tray promised. "But it's not caviar or foie gras or lemon-herbed pastries from the Champagne district of France made with super virgin olive pate. I'll have words with the chef."

Leinani could not help giggling, and she was momentarily confused by the strings of cheese from her oily meal, finally accepting the use of her fingers to wind them up and break them from her lips. "My etiquette teacher didn't cover this eventuality. I'm just not certain which of my forks to use."

"They aren't going to give us forks," Tray scoffed. "We might stab our way out." He seemed to reconsider. "But anyway, it should be the salad fork, because there are tomatoes in the sauce and that qualifies this as a salad."

Tray ate as ravenously as she did, and Leinani had to jerk her gaze away from the way his clean-shaven jaw moved as he chewed to concentrate on her own food.

She was hungry enough that she swiftly finished her pizza pocket and licked her fingers clean. It was a far cry from the state dinner that she might have been expecting, but it stilled the worst of her hunger pangs.

Tray watched her as if he couldn't help himself. "You're going to have to stop doing that," he complained, and Leinani could tell that he was trying to say it lightly.

"Licking my fingers?" she said, and just to be silly, she licked her thumb in his direction.

It backfired terribly, and she was frozen there a moment in the backwash of his desire, her tongue on her thumb like a dog caught with a stolen treat. "Sorry," she said, demurely returning her hand to her lap to use the hand towel and wipe her lips.

"You can't do that," Tray said, strangled. "We have to be more careful."

"I know," she agreed. "I didn't think. I'm so sorry. I only meant to be funny." She couldn't look at him, because he was too handsome and she wanted him too badly.

"It's a freaking minefield," Tray agreed with a sympathetic sigh. "I mean, c'mon, it's going to take all your willpower to resist this much man." He leaned back and put his stockinged feet up on the table, wiggling his toe through the hole at her.

"Stop, stop!" Leinani begged dramatically. "I can't hold myself back! A bare toe! So much *virilité*! I am faint!"

They could both laugh then, and Leinani felt their curious bond resonate with all their conflicted feelings. It was like being in a funhouse, everything she felt magnified and reflected in unfamiliar ways. She couldn't tell what was her own emotion, what was her dragon, what was real, and what was a weird echo from the future.

Possible future.

Possible future that they were going to keep from happening.

They cleaned up their meal and Tray swept up the crumbs from the floor. Suspecting that the laundry service would be unreliable, Leinani washed the hand towels in the bathroom sink using the tiny bar of soap and hung them in the shower to dry. She considered taking a shower herself, but was rather suddenly overcome by exhaustion.

"You're tired," Tray said, suddenly at the open door to the bathroom.

"So are you," she retorted. "It's almost dawn." Outside the window were impressive mountains, forested hills, and a few distant houses. The tops of the mountains were just starting to show color. Nothing looked familiar, and there weren't any signs to give them even a hint at which country they were in.

"Who knows which time zone we're even in," Tray said. "Or how long night is here. There's no point in staying up, at any rate. It would be better if we were well rested."

Better for what? Leinani wondered. Escape? She wished that their mental bond was something other than just a whole lot of jumbled emotion. Being able to speak telepathically would have been useful, or even sharing full pictures of places.

"You should take the bed," Leinani said, before Tray could offer. She wished that there were toothbrushes; her mouth still tasted unpleasantly like cheap pizza. She should have thought to ask for them from Amara. "You're taller, it will be more comfortable."

Tray laughed. "Oh, no, princess. I will take the couch, the bed is yours."

Leinani gave him a narrow-eyed gaze as she passed him coming out of the bathroom. "Is this some machismo thing where you are determined to make the greater sacrifice?"

"Yes," Tray agreed with a grin. "I'm glad you recognized it, so we can get that right out of the way."

"I could get to the couch first," Leinani warned him, feinting in that direction. "You wouldn't dare manhandle me off of it once I'm there."

"Wouldn't I?"

What started as a test of stubbornness almost ended in a crumbling of wills and they both had to turn away to gather their wits, undoubtedly picturing exactly the same manhandling. Leinani wasn't sure what was her rush of desire and what was his, only knew that they both desperately wanted the same thing.

Oh yes, her dragon hissed.

"You can take the couch tonight," she conceded, chin high as she shushed her dragon. "We'll trade off."

"The perfect diplomat," Tray teased her. He didn't argue, but Leinani suspected that the conflict was not actually resolved yet.

There was an extra blanket in the closet, which looked like it would barely cover Tray to his holey sock. He took it, and one of the pillows from the bed, without a word of complaint, then went to lie on the couch while Leinani crept self-consciously into the big, sagging bed and turned off the light. How much more comfortable would it be with Tray here with her, solid and safe to curl up against…

He gave a hiss through the darkness, then said plaintively, "Whatever you're thinking about, you've got to stop that."

"Sorry!" Leinani squeaked. A moment later, she added, "You do, too!"

"Sorry!" Tray groaned.

She couldn't help laughing, and she wasn't sure exactly when she was finally able to slip into exhausted sleep.

12

The couch was as uncomfortable as Tray had feared it would be. The breaks in the cushions were all at exactly the wrong places on his body, it was just short enough that he couldn't quite stretch out, and it was narrow enough that he couldn't curl up sideways.

Eventually he slept anyway, lulled by the comfortable unconsciousness of Leinani in the back of his mind.

When he woke up, for a moment, it was all a dream. Everything that happened was just a blur of impossibility, like houses that weren't quite the houses he knew, with hallways that didn't end and doorways that went to meadows and rooms full of Jell-O. There was no way that the Compact had tapped him. And it certainly hadn't chosen his brother's bride for him. Adding kidnapping seemed like a laughable plot device.

Then he became aware of the cramp in his back, and the fact that his blanket had slipped half off of him. It was warm enough in the room that it didn't particularly matter. It was, in fact, warm enough that Tray thought it would probably be unpleasant if he weren't a dragon, and daylight was bright against his eyelids.

It *had* happened, he realized, opening dry eyes to stabbing light. All of it. He and Leinani had been mistakenly attached at the heart, kidnapped, and were now being held hostage in a dingy little hotel room in some unknown country for some unknown reason. The room smelled like pizza and ant attractant; there were a few traps in the corners, suggesting that the building was home to undesirables other than them.

Tray stretched, dangling his feet off the end of the couch, and felt his joints pop. A flight would be nice, he thought wistfully. He longed to spread his wings.

He felt the moment that Leinani woke, like a bubble had popped in his head. It wasn't unpleasant, having her there. It was just...dangerous, because he liked it a little too much. Because she wasn't supposed to be so comfortable and right. Fask's fiancé, he reminded himself, over his dragon's wordless protest.

Leinani gave a little sigh and Tray felt the same frustration and disappointment that he'd been wrestling with. "I was hoping it was a dream," she murmured, rolling to face him.

"Well, *I'm* undoubtedly the stuff of your dreams," he teased. "But the rest of this is kind of a nightmare. We're still stuck in this seedy hotel room for the moment, and there's no sign of the room service I ordered hours ago."

Leinani's smile was like a tiny beam of sunlight on a cloudy day. "I'm beginning to regret my travel agent for recommending this place."

There was a brisk courtesy knock on the door, the sound of a keycard at the lock, and it opened without invitation. The spell around the room gave a curious, audible little blurble and two new guards walked in, one with a tray of food, one lingering behind with a gun. They were afraid of them, Tray thought. Even unable to shift, they were dragons, stronger and faster than humans, and still dangerous. The idea gave him a certain amount of satisfaction.

They should fear us, his dragon steamed.

The guard put the tray on the desk by the door as Leinani sat up and swung her legs off the bed. They left without conversation, the door giving a little shick of sound as it latched.

Tray went into the bathroom to relieve himself, take his shirt off, and splash cold water over his face; it seemed pointless to shower if there was no clean clothing to put on, and his stomach was grumbling.

He heard Leinani doing...something out in the hotel room, and when he left the bathroom, he found that she had rearranged the room, putting the bed against the wall under the windows and dragging the couch so he had to turn to pass it.

"Interesting interior design choice," Tray observed.

Leinani turned to look at him, then gave a little squeak of dismay at the sight of him shirtless. She had to turn away before she could explain. "It occurred to me that it would be more defensible if people entering the room were funneled this direction. It also gives a blind corner here where we could stage an ambush if necessary. Put some pillows under the blankets on the bed so they think they can see both of us, and one of us stands there. There's still this to get around," Leinani gestured to her necklace without touching it, "but I want to be ready for an opportunity, if it presents itself."

"What the hell do they teach you in princess school?" Tray asked admiringly.

"Oh, you know, back-stabbing, deceit, a little espionage, how to coordinate your accessories, seventeen methods of flirtation." She played with her rings, ducked her head, and fluttered her eyelashes at him.

"Don't do that," Tray begged, not because she looked alluring, but because she looked fun and forward and he wanted to catch her up in his arms and tickle the laugh that was lurking behind her lips right out of her mouth.

She knew exactly what she'd done and Tray watched with regret as she sobered and nodded flustered agreement. "Fine, but you have to put on a shirt," she told him.

"Deal."

She finger-combed her hair, which looked like a considerably harder job than he faced, and frowned down at her rumpled clothing. At least she'd changed from her fancy paper-looking dress to watch the hockey game; she was wearing a silvery-gray pant suit with white embroidery. She had the jacket off, and the undershirt was entirely too flimsy for Tray's peace of mind, but it was better than her bare arms.

Barely.

Tray pulled his own undershirt on, trying to stifle all the feelings that he knew Leinani must be picking up on.

"So, ground rules," he proposed. "I wear a shirt, you don't do that eyelash thing. Or the pout thing. Or the cha cha thing."

"Cha cha thing?"

"With your hips. That swingy way you walk."

"I'm a woman, Tray," she said with exasperation. "That's how I walk."

"It drives me crazy. You're dealing with a hockey player, remember. I can't be expected to manage my baser instincts."

Leinani's mouth twitched. "I shall endeavor to walk sedately and keep my hips from hinging the way that nature meant them to. Anything else?"

"While we're at it, yes. No licking your lips."

Perversely, she did just that.

"Hey!"

"They tasted good."

They would, Tray thought. They would taste amazing. They would taste like flowers or fruit, or maybe spices. They would taste like *her*. The joke went brittle in the air between them, each of them imagining the taste of the other's lips.

"Um, so, they brought us some granola bars, do you want some breakfast?" Leinani's flush was obvious under her tanned cheeks as she turned to the tray that they'd brought. There were some noodle soup cups, a selection of granola bars, and a few individual size packages of nuts.

Tray cleared his throat, and licked his own lips reflexively, not even realizing that he had until Leinani protested, "No lip-licking! That goes both ways."

"Is that supposed to be our breakfast, or our whole day?" Tray asked, strangled, willing his hard-on to subside. It was like being assaulted with desire, and part of him was pleased that it wasn't all just his own.

"We should probably ration it," Leinani said mournfully. "Though I could certainly eat it all right now."

They settled for eating just the granola bars, and cups of individually brewed coffee of highly questionable quality. "I'm surprised they left us the coffee maker," Leinani said, nodding to Tray to put her cup on the table rather than handing it to her in a way that their hands might brush. "We could use water that hot as a weapon."

"Like they used to pour boiling oil on invaders in medieval times?"

She took a sip and wrinkled her nose. "Maybe we could just poison them with this."

Tray sat opposite from her on the floor itself; the coffee

table was so short that it worked better as a dining table if they didn't try sitting on the couch or in the chair. It also helped him pretend that he wasn't still sporting a stiffy.

They ate the meager offerings quietly, each of them carefully focused on their crumbly dry bar and their poor quality coffee. Tray couldn't tell what Leinani was thinking, but he could tell she was trying not to think about him, the same way he was trying not to think about her.

"So, maybe we're going about this the wrong way," he suggested. "You should tell me what habits you hate, so that I can cultivate them and repulse you. I could learn to chew on my fingernails, or loudly burp after meals."

Leinani smiled at him gratefully. He was going to have to add all smiling to the list of things she couldn't do. "I have brothers, too," she reminded him. "Bodily functions aren't going to put me off. I used to regularly win the loudest farting contest after state dinners."

Tray laughed out loud. "I would have figured you for the silent and deadly type," he said frankly. "Being a princess, and all."

"I'm complicated," Leinani said with a chuckle.

The granola bars were long gone, and there was nothing else to do. Leinani fastidiously picked all of the crumbs from her wrapper with her thumb and neatly folded it flat. Tray thought that he caught her aborting a lip-licking.

Tray crumpled his own wrapper, but the resilient material immediately returned to nearly its original shape. "Leinani," he said hesitantly into the quiet moment.

She looked up and met his gaze deliberately for the first time that morning.

"You...don't have to worry about me," he said honestly. "I mean, that stuff about how you walk and whatever you want to do with your tongue. I'm going crazy, and I know that you are, too, but you don't have to wonder if I'm going to do anything you don't want. Or for that matter, anything you do want. I know that you're getting a head full of what I'm feeling, but believe it or not, I can keep my beastly instincts and my irritating housemate of a dragon reined in. You shouldn't have to move a certain way or dress modestly or whatever crap princess school teaches. I won't step out of line, no matter what. You can trust me, and I don't want this to be worse because you feel like it's your sole responsibility to keep us both honest."

Her face softened in a way that Tray hadn't expected or been braced for, making her more beautiful yet as he got a wave of her gratitude and respect.

"That's big of you," she said quietly.

"For a hockey player," Tray added.

"For anyone," Leinani said firmly, and Tray wasn't sure if he'd been scolded, or if she was berating herself. "It won't be easy, but we can get through this. I mean, being kidnapped together wasn't part of the plan, but nothing else has changed. We wait out the spell and I marry your brother. And I'd...like it if we could be friends."

Tray wasn't sure why that hit him harder than anything else she'd said. Why would the idea of being *friends* feel more right than any of the rest of the emotional soup his dragon was augmenting? Maybe the spell was already starting to ease, and they *had* changed their possible future. "Friends," he agreed eagerly. "Just friends." He thrust his hand across the table and she took it for a handshake that was a terrible mistake.

They both snatched their hands back swiftly. "Friends that don't touch," he added.

"No-touch friends," Leinani agreed with a squeak.

Touch... his dragon encouraged.

You are no help at all, Tray replied. *You're the opposite of help.*

13

Leinani knew that she couldn't keep the warm feelings that Tray had released to herself, but she hoped that they seemed only like gratitude and not growing infatuation.

Her first impression of him had been almost purely physical, and layered with what she already knew about him—that he played hockey and was something of a prankster—she had built a picture in her mind of a shallow, even slightly stupid screwup. A really hot screwup, even hotter when he flashed her one of those devastating playful smiles, but completely not her type.

But her type, it turned out, was someone who had puppy-chewed holes in his socks, who could make her laugh with fart jokes, with unexpected depths and a solid sense of chivalry that Leinani thought was only found in fiction.

Someone was going to be lucky to have him, eventually.

Not someone, her dragon protested. *Us. Ours.*

"So, what are we supposed to do while they get around

to doing whatever it is they are going to do with us?" she asked, to distract herself. "There's no television or radio, no books, no games. I doubt they're going to let us out for a walk."

"We could play I Spy," Tray suggested. "Granola bar wrapper origami?" He smoothed his wrapper and started folding it. It immediately unfolded.

"I spy, with my little eye, something that starts with B," Leinani started.

"Boring," Tray guessed. "Bored. Boy?"

Leinani shook her head.

"Blind corner?"

"No, but you're very close."

Tray looked around the room, paused at the windows, and then exclaimed, "Blinds!"

Leinani clapped her hands, and her tiny feeling of delight was like a drug rush.

Before Tray could take a turn, there was another knock, and the little click-click of the keycard at the door. It was a cautious, Slavic-looking woman, holding a small stack of clothing with two pairs of canvas boat shoes perched on top. She was followed by two alert-looking guards they hadn't seen before, just as young and eager looking as the first pair. They all looked at the new room configuration curiously, and the maid put the clothing on the desk.

"Thank you!" Leinani said, standing up from the couch to smile at them. "And please, could you let me know if we should be expecting a lunch or if this...?"

"Fresh towels?" Tray added hopefully.

They all turned and left without comment, leaving Leinani to trail off. The maid looked genuinely afraid.

"Well, that was unfriendly," Tray complained. "But right now, a shower and clean clothes sounds pretty nearly as good as a seven course meal. You can go first, if you'd like."

He said it courteously, but Leinani wasn't fooled. "You go first," she insisted. "I'm not the one who smells like a hockey player."

"You keep thinking that, princess," he teased, but rather than argue, he vaulted easily over the back of the couch and rifled the pile of clothing, then disappeared into the bathroom with a selection from it.

Leinani went around the couch more sedately, and stood at the table sorting what was left, trying very hard not to think about Tray stripping off his clothing. He was going to need a *very* cold shower.

The clothing was quaintly secondhand, except for the underthings—a package of solid color briefs for Tray and bikini cut underwear for her, and a single pack of cheap white sports socks they must be meant to share. There was no bra, but Leinani supposed that would be more complicated to size. There were a handful of unisex T-shirts that were going to be big on her and small on Tray, and a pair of jeans that, when she held them out, looked like it ought to fit Leinani if she wore a belt to cinch in the waist.

The shoes were in two sizes, and the smallest was going to be comically large on her. Leinani suspected she would just go barefoot, as she often did at home.

Then, abruptly, she had to put both her hands on the desk and breathe hard. She might have been mostly successful in keeping herself from wantonly imagining Tray, nude and covered in bubbles, but he was apparently not being as careful, or possibly he had just...paid attention to certain parts in his soaping, because she was rather suddenly on absolute fire.

How terrible would it be to touch herself? Would it relieve any of the tension, or would it just make things yet more awkward? Leinani could barely *think* through the wash of desire and need that was crawling her skin.

She was standing close enough to the bathroom door to hear Tray swear, though she couldn't make out his words, then her libido was rapidly quenched as he gave the faucet a wrench and turned the water to full cold. His shock and discomfort shook Leinani out of her own reverie.

When he finally emerged, he was wearing his new-old clothes and looked, Leinani thought furiously, like a rock star. His jeans were almost obscenely tight. Still damp, his hair stuck up wildly, and he was scowling like a storm cloud.

"My turn," Leinani said, too loudly in the uncomfortably quiet room. She should ask Amara about a radio. Or some kind of music player, if their captors didn't want them listening to broadcasts. She took an armload of clothing, then realized that the pinch point she had so brilliantly designed into the room had backfired terrible.

Tray stared at her, his expression as naked longing as hers.

"Excuse me," she said with effort, clutching her clothing, and she pulled herself to the side so that he could get past without touching.

He stood a moment longer, looking hungrily at her, then squeezed past, rubbing against the rough-plastered wall in his effort to stay as far away as possible.

Leinani slammed the door behind her harder than she meant to.

The bathroom was very basic. It had a long counter with a foolishly shallow sink on one side, and a bathtub with a shower curtain around it on the other, with a toilet at the far end. A mirror over the sink showed Leinani a fogged reflection. It was probably just as well; she knew she must look a fright. She would have to ask Amara for a hairbrush, she thought. She turned on the shower and wearily undressed, then crawled into the bathtub and sat down in the stream of lukewarm water to cry helplessly.

It was too much. It was too hard.

She'd gone to Alaska to make a state marriage, one that she had hoped wouldn't be too onerous. Fask was a good man, she was a dutiful daughter; she thought she could be happy and find purpose. And instead, she'd been enchanted by a misplaced spell to the wrong prince, and after a night of pretending that everything was just fine, she'd been captured, kidnapped by a madwoman, and trapped with the one man that she wanted more than anything and couldn't have.

Worst of all was knowing that Tray must be gritting his teeth through her pitiful breakdown, hopelessly amplified through their dragons.

Leinani stood carefully, tipping her head up into the water to let it wash away her tears. No more of that, she told herself. She found a tiny bottle of shampoo and used it to wash not only her hair, but her body, keeping herself woodenly on task as she efficiently washed and rinsed and turned off the cool water.

It will pass, she tried to reassure herself. It won't be this bad forever.

She dried as carefully as she had washed, then wrapped the towel around her wet hair. There was a cradle on the wall for an electric hair dryer, but it had been removed, the cord cut at the wall.

She started to get dressed, then realized that she had forgotten a key component of her clothing outside the bathroom: her underpants.

14

The cold shower had not done as much as Tray had hoped it would to cool his libido. He thought fixedly about hockey, about dog sledding, about dips in icy lakes...and he inevitably came back around to the way Leinani's cheek had felt when he touched her, and the way she looked the times that he made her laugh.

He hoped that she would have better luck with her shower than he had, because he was very sure he'd done her no favors, and could feel how tightly wound she was, echoing all his own conflict and craving.

It's getting crowded in here, he remarked to his dragon.

Then Leinani's grief washed over him and he nearly barged into the bathroom without thinking, stopping at the very last moment. He flattened his palm on the door and leaned against it, desperate to comfort her and helpless. He stood that way for a long moment, then slid down to sit against it. He couldn't hear her crying over the sound of the running water through the thick door, but he knew that she was, and it tore him up inside like shards of glass.

All he could do was sit against the door and wrestle

with all his own feelings of despair and frustration. *It will go away,* he tried to convince himself. They would escape, or be rescued, and all of this complication would just vanish.

He was trying so hard not to make Leinani feel worse that he didn't notice when she finished her shower, and fell into the bathroom when she opened the door behind him.

She was only wearing a towel, and Tray was nearly lying on the floor.

"I'm sorry," he said, scrambling to his feet. "I'm sorry. I wasn't...eavesdropping. I was just...you were sad."

"It's been a rough couple of days. Twenty-four hours. Whatever it's been," she said, looking ashamed.

"Don't feel bad," Tray begged, and he realized that he was trapping them in a terrible emotional loop with his guilt. "It's not your fault."

"It's not yours, either," Leinani was quick to counter. "I just...I need my underthings."

"Oh," Tray said, and they were both very keenly aware of how little she was wearing. "Let me get those—" he said, just as she said, "Maybe I should—"

He got to the desk first, and handed her the plastic-wrapped package as Leinani tried to stride too far and nearly exposed herself. "Thank you," she squeaked, clutching the towel in one hand in the underpants in the other. She backed into the bathroom door handle, snagging her towel as she dashed back.

It undoubtedly would have given Tray a brief show if he hadn't hauled himself around to look the other way with every inch of his self control before the towel could fall.

Tray went to the window and stared out. When he tentatively touched the glass, he could feel the spell flex warningly under his fingers and his necklace seemed to heat. He resisted the temptation to test his threshold of pain, not wanting to inflict it on Leinani.

After a while, he found a crumpled granola bar wrapper and amused himself tossing it back and forth to himself.

"What is that sound?" Leinani asked, when she came out of the bathroom at last, marginally safer to look at with an oversized t-shirt and a pair of jeans, her hair still damp around her shoulders. She came past the couch but didn't volunteer to go too close to the window. There was a lull in the sounds of machinery; the heater was quiet, and there was, for the moment, no water running in adjacent rooms.

Tray caught his wrapper and held it still.

Distantly, there was a curious far-off murmur.

"It sounds like, I don't know...chanting?" Tray said, not able to hide his unease.

"How...cliché," Leinani murmured. "Will there be screaming next? Perhaps some ritual sacrifice?"

They were quiet for a while, listening to the ebb and flow of the far-off voices. Then some kind of droning machine above them kicked on, and the sounds were drowned out completely in a sea of white noise that they hadn't even noticed before.

Leinani dragged her hand along one wall, testing the response of the spell and the burn at her own throat.

Tray resumed tossing the wrapper to himself idly.

They orbited the room in careful circles, restlessly, always keeping distance between them.

"Hockey," Leinani said abruptly. "Will you tell me about hockey?"

Tray nearly lost control of the wrapper, leaning to catch it with his long arm outstretched. "Hockey?" He closed his hand around the makeshift ball. It seemed like a safe enough subject.

"Well, my usual sports of swimming and surfing and diving aren't going to translate well to living in the middle of a giant block of ice," Leinani pointed out. "I should learn to do something the locals do. But I watched a game on television and realized that there was more to it than just hitting a puck back and forth. They kept blowing the whistle and I couldn't figure out why. I mean, once it was obvious, when there were two guys out there pounding on each other, but most of the time I couldn't make sense of it."

"Icing," Tray explained. "The purpose is to keep the puck in play, not just toss it back and forth down the rink with no one around it. That's boring. So, if it crosses too many blue lines without someone controlling it, it's blown dead."

He put his wrapper down on the coffee table. "Okay, if this is your rink, you'll have a goal here, and one here. Oh, let's see." The two pairs of shoes became goal posts, their laces the lines, and Tray filled her in on the rules and explained puck drops and penalties and power plays. He relaxed a little as they talked, and felt her do the same.

They devolved to playing a modified tabletop game of something that barely resembled hockey, taking turns trying to get the granola bar wrapper through the opposing shoe goal with a very inadequate coffee stir stick. Leinani danced her triumph when she scored, and Tray made a show of shaking his fists in mock frustration, even though he had already scored on her a dozen times.

"You'd be a brutal opponent," Tray said. "Relentless and fast."

"I'd fall on my ass the moment my skates touched ice," Leinani assured him. "I'll leave that for you. But at least now I can cheer for the Alaska team and yell at the refs without looking like a complete idiot."

Tray had to smile at her bemusedly. He had trouble imagining her yelling at a ref.

"Tell me about something you do," Tray invited. "Do you play a sport?" He had to squash the idea of Leinani in a short-skirted tennis outfit stretching to hit a ball with a racquet.

"Not team sports, so much," Leinani said. "But I love to surf."

"That looks really hard to do," Tray observed.

"Says the guy who walks around on ice wearing knives strapped to his boots," Leinani pointed out. "It's just a matter of keeping your gravity low, and knowing the ocean."

She spoke lovingly about the water, about watching the waves and swimming with turtles and sun-drying on the beach.

"It seems like it must have been hard to leave your island," Tray said. "It sounds like paradise."

Complicated, was the only way to describe what she felt about that. As Tray tried to define the strands of emotion out of the jumble she was feeling, she hesitantly said, "I wasn't really important there. My mother was queen, my brother's mate was crown princess. I thought...I could be useful in Alaska. I mean, your brothers have mates, but they're..."

"American peasants?" Tray guessed.

Leinani laughed. "I don't mean to disparage them," she said, and he could feel her chagrin. "Not that at all. It's just...neither seemed interested in the spotlight. And it's not that I personally love it, it's just that was something I actually know how to do, and I...wanted to do something I'm good at. Be something important. Do something that mattered." She looked down at her hands. "I guess that sounds kind of shallow."

"No," Tray said immediately. "I know exactly how you feel." He was able to turn it into a quick joke by pointing at his head. "Like, literally."

When the sun seemed highest in the hazy sky, they used the coffee machine to make the noodle soup. They hadn't been given any utensils with the cups, so they drank the broth and slurped the noodles like barbarians, using their coffee stir sticks to get the last bits out. The last few inches were intensely salty and flavored.

Somehow, it was one of the most weirdly satisfying meals that Tray had ever eaten, even though he ended it still hungry. They both licked their fingers at the end, caught each other doing it, and laughed themselves giddy.

They were hysterical, Tray thought. Everything was slightly surreal and terribly funny because that was the only way that their brains had to cope with the stress.

There were no napkins, so they used the same hand towels from the day before, and Tray scooped them up before Leinani could. "You washed them up last time," he pointed out.

He was still in the bathroom wringing them out when the door made that snick-snick sound of the keycard that set his heart racing anxiously.

Tray came out of the bathroom to find Leinani turned around on the couch for a view of the door; the biggest downside to the new rearrangement of the room was that they would sit with their backs to the door. Maybe Leinani could convince them to bring in a second couch with her womanly wiles. A longer couch, or a fold-out, since Tray actually had no intention of rotating between the bed and the couch.

The door opened on a woman with a pile of towels. Guards lurked directly behind her but didn't offer to come in.

"Oh, we get towel service!" he said jovially. "Best kidnapping ever."

The woman looked for a moment like she was going to throw the towels at Tray and flee.

Leinani swiftly said, "Pardon me! Could we also get a little more food? And a toothbrush?" She mimed brushing her teeth. "Perhaps some games, or a television?" She smiled winningly. "I've used all the shampoo."

The maid looked at her blankly, shook her head and murmured something in...was it Greek? Possibly Russian. She put the towels down and backed out.

Leinani called to the guards, "A board game would be delightful! A pack of cards?" She laughed and spread her hands. "There's not much damage we could do with a pack of cards!"

"A pad of paper and a pen so we can play tic-tac-toe?" Tray added hopefully.

Then they were gone and the latch of the door was clicking shut with a sound that Tray was sure would cause his stomach to drop forever.

15

"Do you have any idea where we are?" Leinani asked, gazing out the window. They had to take turns in the only space with a view; the bed in its current orientation filled most of the wall with the windows and it was far, far too dangerous for them to stand close together. Tray was bouncing his granola wrapper off the wall and catching it.

"I thought maybe Crete," Tray said. "We traced Amara to the island after Rian threw an ice bucket at her. But I didn't think that Crete got snow, or had mountains."

Leinani had to admit, "I don't know anything about Crete. Beyond the very obvious. It is not, of course, part of the Small Kingdoms. It was once part of Greece but is now independent, it has a parliamentary democracy, the primary industries are tourism and agriculture. Olives, grapes, and carob, I believe."

"Oh, but you don't know anything about Crete," Tray teased her.

Leinani felt herself flush. "It was just…"

"You weren't supposed to feel bad," Tray protested. "You're...really smart. I was trying to compliment you."

"Sorry," Leinani said quietly, not sure what to do with his feelings of remorse or her own feelings of guilt. "I...thank you."

"I didn't have years of princess school," Tray said sheepishly. "I spent more time dodging my tutors or trying to convince them that I was Rian than learning from them."

They were silent a moment, both staring out at the window. He was standing, she was curled up on the bed. The view looked a little like she'd imagined Alaska would, before she actually saw it. The mountains were tall, and had snowy skirts down to a muted green valley. The trees were less lush than the ones she was used to, but considerably larger than the Alaskan spruces. These were pines, she thought, but she didn't know much about any northern trees. She didn't volunteer the information, not sure how to assure Tray that she had already figured out that he was smarter than he let on, or possibly smarter than he believed.

The houses, spaced periodically through the forest, were too distant to make much out on. The building they were in appeared to be at the top of a cliff over a forested chasm; the view below was only treetops, with the barest glimpse of a far-off road. It was hard to tell anything about the building they were in. Leinani guessed that it was several stories high at least, and the lack of sounds of other people above them indicated that they were probably on the top story.

She looked up suddenly.

The ceiling was quite high, and when she bounced up on the bed and reached for it, her hand was still a good foot below the pebbled surface. "Lift me up!" she commanded Tray.

Tray caught her implication immediately. "You think they didn't spell the ceiling?"

If they could break up *through* the roof...

The bed groaned as Tray stepped up onto it and reached up. His hand didn't quite touch, either. He looked down at Leinani. "I, ah..."

Leinani swallowed, already regretting her command. "Sorry I'm not...uh...lighter. People always expect Moana and I'm a lot more Maui, instead." She flexed an arm.

Tray blinked and then gave a burst of laughter. "You're fine, I was just...worried about the...touching." He bent and took Leinani around the waist, hitching her easily up and lifting her into the air.

For a moment, all Leinani could think about was his hands, his strength, how much more of him she wanted on her. His shoulders under her own hands were so broad and strong. His fingers gripped harder. She forced herself to let go and reach up, and when her hand brushed the ceiling, the tense moment shattered into agony.

They collapsed down onto the bed, Tray catching her and rolling as she spasmed and cried out.

It was a moment before the light of the pain cleared enough to make out Tray, an arm on either side of her as he looked down at her in worry. "Don't do that again," he begged.

"Duly noted," she agreed breathlessly.

For a moment, she thought he was going to kiss her, and she dearly wished that he would.

Then he made a noise that echoed her own dragon's grumble of frustration and pulled himself off of her and off the bed altogether. Leinani lay limply in the aftermath of her pain, eyes closed, until there was a courtesy knock at the door.

Whoever was there waited considerably longer than their other visitors had without barging in, and finally Leinani called, "Come in," as she pulled her ill-fitting jeans into place again and stood up. They probably wouldn't give her a belt or a safety pin.

It was the same woman who had brought them the towels earlier, and the same guards. She had a pile of boxes that Leinani realized were battered board games, and a basket full of what looked like vending machine rejects.

"Oh, bless your heart," Leinani said in joy.

The uncommunicative woman left without comment, leaving the pile at the desk behind the couch. Leinani had planned to incorporate the desk into her sitting area, perhaps getting rid of the shin-biting coffee table, but now she thought that perhaps it was more useful to leave it where it was.

Tray took the pile of games to the coffee table while Leinani brought the basket over the back of the couch. It contained more granola bars, some individual bags of chips and nuts, a cello-wrapped pastry, and one chocolate bar. Some of the packaging was in English, one was in Chinese or Japanese, and one… "This could be Greek," Leinani said thoughtfully.

Tray agreed, then squealed like a little boy, clutching one of the boxes. "Look what they have! The Dating Game from the seventies!" In a falsetto, he declared, "I am going to get the very cutest date of all. He'll pick me up in his Speedster and we'll hit the mall!"

"That's an actual game?" Leinani said incredulously. "It looks terrible." The box was almost in pieces and badly faded. Someone had drawn mustaches on all the models on the cover.

The other games were Scrabble, and Parcheesi. The box and instructions for Parcheesi were all in Spanish. "I don't know the rules to this game. What does it say?" Tray asked her.

"I don't know Spanish," Leinani said in surprise.

He was as surprised as she was. "You don't? I thought all those islands spoke Spanish."

"Spanish islands do," she said, slowly smiling. "Mostly in the Atlantic. But Mo'orea is down there by the French Polynesia islands. I speak French. And Tahitian. And a little German."

"Oh, only a little German, pffff..."

He was impressed with her again. And feeling stupid again. If she hadn't known what he was feeling, his expression of casual indifference might have fooled her. She grudgingly admitted that however much the Compact was on her least favorite list right now, if it was going to attach two people for its ulterior purposes, having them cut to the chase by sharing emotions was remarkably effective.

A little too effective.

She liked the man behind the screw-up impression and the jokes. Knowing what he was really feeling made everything dangerously intimate. She would never be fooled by his deprecation or his carelessness; she knew now how sensitive and smart he was beneath all of his bluster, and how unexpectedly deep. She was starting to see the tiny physical cues that she'd never have otherwise picked up on.

"I wish we had our cellphones," Leinani said. "I never realized how much I used mine until I didn't have it. I could just look up the rules online."

"Or call home." Tray rifled through the basket of

vending machine castoffs. "Or we could get delivery of some decent food."

"Want to play a game of Scrabble?" she suggested. "Winner takes the chocolate bar?"

"You are on, princess."

Leinani thought at first that Tray was going to throw the game in her favor because there was something cagey about the way that he felt, but when she opened with TEMPT, he threw himself into the game with gusto. He extended it to TEMPTRESS and his poker face was unconvincing.

Giggling, Leinani spun a TACT down from there, just missing a triple letter score. He took it with a modest COW. "What on earth are you trying to say about me?" Leinani teased, giving him a mock glare.

"Clearly that you are a *temptress cow*," he laughed at her. "But at least you're tactful."

"Well, you are definitely a W-A-S-T-E," Leinani said, claiming the triple letter score beneath it.

"I am wounded!" Tray exclaimed, clutching his heart. Then he added an S to it and used the triple word space to put in WISHES for an impressive number of points.

"You are destroying me!" Leinani protested, looking at her board of nearly all low-value vowels. "I can't make anything with these."

"Turn 'em in or turn it up, your highness," Tray mocked.

"ATE," Leinani said, returning to the original word to dump some of her vowels. She drew an X and an S.

Tray put an F at the top of her word, which gave them both a moment of pause and stretched FIGHT off of it for entirely too many points, the G landing on a triple letter score.

Fighting fate in several different ways, Leinani tried to

rearrange the letters on her board to spell anything worth points but the very obvious SEXY, which would land on a double word score.

She glanced at him, then laughed helplessly and played the word. There was no point in trying to hide her chagrin, not with him.

Tray wolf-whistled, but Leinani thought his cheeks looked flushed, and both of them were feeling impossibly tightly strung.

"I did not realize that Scrabble would be such a fraught game," he admitted, looking at his letters.

"I thought it would be an improvement over The Dating Game," Leinani agreed sheepishly. "Clearly I was wrong."

"Clearly."

Leinani could feel his resolve, which was a very curious —and on top of that, a curiously *familiar*—feeling. It gave her hope. They really could get through this...and escape...without losing their battle. They could just be friends.

She made the mistake of remembering how it felt to have him just above her on the bed, and how his shoulders felt under her hands. Friends that didn't touch, she reminded herself, hauling her thoughts back with effort.

No-touch friends.

16

Tray stroked his jaw. A few days of captivity, and he already looked like an unwashed gold prospector, covered with stubble. The guards had not so much denied his request for a razor—even a safety razor!—as simply ignored it, so apparently he was doomed to a jaw-rug. It was itchy, and he hated it.

"I've got to use that room, too!" Leinani reminded him from outside the bathroom. "Quit mooning over your reflection and share the space!"

"I thought they were supposed to teach you things like patience and grace in princess school," Tray retorted through the closed door. "Wait your turn!"

"I have to pee," she protested.

"My illusions about your ladylike manners are swiftly crumbling!" he teased her. He splashed cold water over his scruffy face and ran his fingers through his hair. "Coming, your highness."

They switched places, skirting each other carefully in the narrow space. They were getting good at using the small space they'd been allotted. Leinani had proved stoic in the face of their terrible and irregular meals; they periodically got actual sandwiches and cheap take-out without distinguishing wrappers, but they kept a few packages of nuts in reserve for the times that food simply didn't show up.

"It's like they don't even always remember that we're here," she observed.

They did their laundry by hand and hung it in the shower to dry, rotating through what little they had, and they were, at least, well-stocked in tiny hotel shampoo bottles. Leinani had almost cried with joy when a maid brought two cheap toothbrushes and a few squeeze-tube samples of toothpaste.

They played board games, making up their own rules when they didn't know them, or they discovered too many parts missing. They played I Spy, and when all of it seemed uninspiring and too dull to bear, they lay on the floor with their feet on the furniture, not facing each other, and talked about their families. Her brothers and his seemed to have a lot in common, and she told wistful stories about the reefs and mountains of her home. He told her in return about dog sledding through winter forests, and flying over herds of caribou that looked like swarms of ants on the tundra slopes.

His first sight of her, Tray thought she was all princess, proper and pretty, and couldn't imagine why he'd ever feel the things his possible future insisted he would.

But a few days of slumming it, and he could see what earthy, resilient stuff she was made of. She was smart and she was kind, even more than she was beautiful. She could even rein in the errant feelings they had, and every day he was a little more in awe of her sheer strength of spirit.

When she came out of the bathroom, he made himself stop thinking about her. She was tying her hair back in a ponytail; there had been a few rubber bands in their last food delivery and she'd been as delighted as if they had been jeweled hair clips. "If we stopped up the toilet, do you think we could get someone in here that we could use as a hostage to get out?" she suggested.

"It's not a bad idea," Tray said. "But there are still these to get around." He touched the string choker that had become a familiar part of his reflection and winced at the sizzle. He'd spent some time testing to see if he could build an immunity to it, until Leinani begged him tearfully to stop. He could handle shocking himself, but he couldn't bear bringing her pain.

"You're right," Leinani agreed. "And I get the feeling that most of these people are brainwashed into believing that they are ready to throw their lives away for Dear Leader Amara, so I'm not sure how good a hostage any of them would actually be."

"Plus, there'd be that whole inconvenience of not having a toilet to use while they fix it," Tray pointed out. "If they fix it!"

"Okay, not my greatest plan yet," Leinani agreed, not —to Tray's relief—feeling more than the tiniest bit bad about it. "I'm just really sick of the service at this place. It's so not up to my usual standards." Sometimes, she adopted that haughty princess voice and stance just to make him smile.

He did that now, marveling over how different she looked with her long dark hair pulled back. He had just finally gotten better at not staring at her constantly, and now she looked completely different and more gorgeous than ever.

They both jerked their gazes away at the same time. Even hockey wasn't a safe train of thought, because Leinani wanted to know more about the sport and they played competitive games with trash and temporary goals that sometimes set his blood on fire, watching her dive to block his scores.

A knock on the door had them both alert. It was late night, the windows already dark and the sky showing just a little glow over the mountains. It was much later than they usually got any visitors.

"Come in," Leinani called, using her formal company voice.

The guards that came in were much more business than usually, and they had their guns out and ready, not just casually at their sides the way they usually did. There were also four of them.

"Amara wants to see you." It was the scoffing guard from their first day.

"We would be happy to entertain her," Leinani said, her voice suspiciously close to sarcastic. "I'll get out the best china and serve us all tea."

"Not you," the guard said. "Just him."

Leinani's alarm for him was like being stabbed in the side. If they'd been standing closer, Tray might have reached out and tried to take her hand; they'd gotten in the habit of keeping as much space between them as they could because of their terrible instincts.

Whatever Amara had been working on that required a dragon, it was done, and Tray was filled with dread and fear, and not at all sure how much of it was his own.

"I'll go," he said, lifting his hands in surrender. "You don't have to point those things at her."

He edged around the coffee table that he hadn't quite gotten used to; he had several bruises on his shins from the beastly thing. Leinani, out of habit, melted back to give him plenty of space. If the guards ever wondered why they were usually on opposite sides of the room from each other, they had never speculated out loud.

"C'mon, your *highness*." If Leinani had been suspiciously sarcastic, this guy was dripping in it, and he clearly liked being the one in charge. "Amara's waiting in the control room."

Tray slowed defiantly. "What, no litter to carry me? Where are the trumpets?"

Leinani gave a hiss of warning that Tray felt as much as he felt.

"Let's go." One of the other guards, silent until then, used the tip of his gun to prod him.

Tray refrained from giving him a lecture on proper weapon etiquette and gave a theatrical sigh. "Fine, let's go see Amara."

"Wait!" Leinani cried then, vaulting over the back of the couch.

Tray was just able to turn and catch her as she hurtled herself at him, completely unexpectedly, throwing one of her arms up around his neck as he instinctively bent to catch her. The guards seemed as surprised as he was and made no move to stop her.

At first, Tray was simply overwhelmed by having her close, finally holding her, feeling the soft strength of her up against him. "Leinani," he murmured, burying his face in her hair. She still managed to smell like tropical flowers, after days in their hotel prison.

Then he realized that she was twisting to press something into one of his hands. "It's a listening device," she whispered near his ear, nuzzling close to his neck as if she couldn't bear to see him go. "Try to hide it somewhere out of sight, where it can still pick up sound. Under a desk, or behind something, not muffled in a pocket or a drawer."

It was a ring, Tray realized, not her engagement ring, but one of the etched silver ornaments that she always wore. "Clever princess," he said breathlessly back. It was hard to think clearly with her pressed up to him, her breath at his ear, her warm body against him. His mouth hungered to touch the bronze skin of her bare neck, the slope of her shoulder...surely one kiss would be safe, merely to complete the false embrace she had started to fool the guards.

It was a terrible mistake, he realized at once, as his lips just grazed the place where neck met shoulder. She whimpered and clutched desperately at him. Tray nearly dropped the ring being passed between them, spasming in the collision of desire and duty. His brother's bride, he reminded himself, not his, and helpless rage washed over him.

As gently as he could manage, he slipped the ring onto his little finger as far as it would go and folded his hand tight, then set Leinani carefully away from him.

"Sorry," she mouthed at him, and he only knew what she was saying because it was the same thing he was thinking.

Sorry.

Sorry that she wasn't his. Sorry that she was supposed to marry his brother. Sorry that they were stuck together despite themselves. Sorry, at times, that they'd ever met at all.

"Sorry to break up the beautiful moment, lovebirds," Scoff said firmly. "Let's go."

Tray went obediently, offering no further jokes as he turned away from Leinani. She gave a sharp little intake of breath, not quite a sob and it took all his willpower not to turn back and comfort her.

He stalked ahead of Scoff and Whiny as if he was the one leading the interrogation, and he felt the spell around their room drag at him a little, as if it wasn't quite sure he was supposed to leave, but it wasn't sure it should stop him, either. He filed that away as something useful. Spells, like all magic, had rules. He just had to figure out what they were and lawyer his way out of them.

Then he was out of the room that their world had shrunk to and staring down a dim-lit hotel hallway. Scoff prodded him to the left, where a glint at the end suggested a dark, far-off window.

Tray guessed that he and Leinani had been put in the finest room of the bunch by the spacing between the doors, for what that was worth, and he also suspected that it was not actively being used as a hotel. There was no sign of other guests, only a few scattered men wearing mismatched military gear. He counted doors, not sure what he'd do with the information, but grateful to have *something* to do at last.

He walked past the door he'd been meant to turn at and Scoff took the opportunity to take him roughly by the elbow. He was the largest of the goons and while Tray was sure he could break free of his grip, it wouldn't have been without a struggle. He eyed the window at the end of the hall, thought about the necklace at his throat, about Leinani, still trapped, and the ring that she'd slipped him, halfway down his smallest finger.

He offered Scoff no trouble and turned into the indicated room.

It had the same mid-rate hotel layout with a narrow hall past a pedestrian bathroom that opened into a spartan suite. It looked like a mirror of the room he was sharing with the princess.

Tray glanced around swiftly, cataloging the position of the windows, anything nearby that might be a weapon, and especially the people, keeping half an eye out for a good place to squirrel Leinani's ring away.

There were no beds in this room, only a few couches and a ring of folding tables with computers and a series of monitors that showed a grid of security cameras. He had only a moment to take in the subjects—there was the door of his own prison, and what must be the entrance of the building, and...he frowned at the far monitor. It looked like a classroom, with rows of children at desks, their heads bent over their work. They seemed to range in age between a child of about eight and several that might have been adults. It felt late for a class to be in session.

Amara was standing at the window. There were lights out of this window, like a distant small town, and a dark expanse past it that might have been ocean.

"We've got the dragon prince for you," Whine started.

The woman who had been working at the keyboard looked up and with a keystroke, the monitors went dark. She had a crown of tight strawberry-blonde braids around her head and she was thin and looked young.

There were three guards, besides his own, and they wore the same nondescript clothing that Whiny and Scoff did. They weren't actively holding their guns, but they all looked capable of violence, given the chance. Tray couldn't pin down why they gave him such a creepy feeling. Maybe their entranced expressions?

None of them would have stood a chance against him if he'd been able to shift. Tray resisted the urge to tug at the string around his neck. He'd learned that lesson.

"Well," Amara said, turning and looking at him appraisingly. "Let's see if this works."

"My family will pay handsomely for our safe return," Tray said. "If that's what you're looking for."

Amara laughed. "No, prince, you know that is not at all what I am looking for."

"Political leverage, then?"

Amara gave him a pitying look, as if he was a very simple child and Tray reminded himself that he didn't care if some crazy kidnapper thought he was dumb. Leinani thought he was smart, he reminded himself.

"I'm not interested in that kind of power," she said, shaking her head. "I want *your* power."

Tray was confused, and made no attempt to hide it. "What are you babbling on about?"

Amara was turning, apparently not interested in providing the villain monologue that he'd been half-hoping for. "Buckle him in."

The guards hustled him to a sturdy chair, bolted down to the floor, that had restraints at the ankle and wrist, and they strapped him in a little rougher than Tray thought was strictly necessary.

"It's ready, Mackenzie?" Amara wanted to know, directing her question at the woman at the computer.

Mackenzie stood and passed Amara a piece of paper that Tray immediately recognized as the same sort of spell that had been captured when Amara had made her unsuccessful attempt to steal the pages the Compact.

"The directives?" Amara wanted to know.

"Press it to his skin and say pull," the woman said. "Hold the vessel with your opposite hand."

"In English?"

"English."

"You're sure?" Amara confirmed. "You saw what happened to Henry."

Mackenzie nodded crisply. "Pull, in English. Skin contact required." She hesitantly asked, "Do you want me to do it, Amara?"

Tray was astonished to watch Amara suddenly soften and put a hand onto the other woman's shoulder. "What kind of leader would I be if I was willing to put the dangerous parts on a follower, Mackenzie? It is my responsibility to do this. You are brave to offer, and that will be remembered." Amara squared herself as if she was facing something that required great resolve and bravery and turned back to Tray with the paper in both hands.

"What the hell are you planning to do?" Tray demanded.

"Should they gag him, Leader, ah, Amara?"

"We should gather as much data as possible," she replied, closing the distance. "Let's see if he screams."

Tray was able to make the restraints creak as he struggled against them, but they had clearly been made with respect for his dragon strength. "What are you going to do?" he asked again.

"Remove his shirt," Amara commanded.

Mackenzie stepped briskly up and began unbuttoning his shirt. Tray's struggles only meant that one of the buttons popped off instead of being released.

Then the paper was being held to his skin in one of Amara's hands. He couldn't feel the fingers that were missing, but he could feel the warmth of the paper as she said, "Pull!" and the spell began to burn through it.

The paper fell into ash.

Tray waited for pain, for something dramatic, and was briefly relieved when the flash of the spell releasing seemed to be too brief to burn him.

Then there was a curious rush underneath his skin, a weird feeling like water running beneath ice and he was...somehow different than he'd been.

Amara drew her hand away in wonder, rubbing her fingers over the gritty ash. "Did it work?" she asked. For the first time, Tray saw what was in her opposite hand, a short, serrated dagger.

"Did what work?" Tray asked in dismay. He felt off, like he was flying even though he knew that his feet were still strapped to the legs of the iron chair. Dizzy, he realized. This is what dizzy felt like.

"Did it cause you pain?" Amara wanted to know. "Were you discomforted at all?" She was clinical again, every inch a scientist. "It is important to document things accurately whenever possible."

"I'm fine," Tray said distantly, surprised by the sound of his own voice. "Never better."

It was a lie, but Tray couldn't have said how he was wrong. Everything was just a little off, like he was a circle when all his life he'd been a square.

What's happening? he asked his dragon in alarm. Dragons were better attuned to magic than humans; surely he would understand what was happening.

Only silence answered him and Tray suddenly understood his odd weakness, and why his skin was uncomfortable in the cool room.

His dragon was gone.

It was as if the strings attaching them had been clipped, like he was muscles and skin without a skeleton.

Panic washed over him. He'd never been alone in his own head before and it took him a moment to realize that he still wasn't.

Leinani wasn't anything like his dragon, but she was there in the same places, desperately worried and, for the moment, the steadiest thing in his life. She loved him. No, she would love him. She might love him. She *could have* loved him. It all blurred together in a helpless swirl of hope.

His sensitivity to her feelings was weaker than it had

been, as if his dragon had been amplifying her, but she was still there.

"Oh, yes," Amara said, lifting the dagger with a gleam in her eye. "Oh, *yes.*"

Her assistant, Mackenzie, only looked nervous.

"Return him to the room," Amara said crisply. "We don't need him to continue the tests."

The guards unbuckled him carefully and Tray clenched his hand as he stood up, alarmed by the feeling of weakness in all his limbs. The listening ring Leinani had slipped to him was still miraculously perched on the first joint of his finger. Clever Leinani.

Leinani. Brave, beautiful Leinani...who was also a dragon.

"Wait," Tray said, staggering towards the computer desk. "Wait!"

To his chagrin, the guards overpowered him at once. He made them work for it; his muscles were honed by hours of hockey playing and running dogs, but he didn't have dragon strength and the two of them were more than a match. His arms were still pinned and they began to drag him out.

Amara halted them. "What is it, your *highness*?" she asked. She looked smug,

"Promise you won't do this to Leinani," Tray said honestly. "Whatever you want, whatever you have to do, do it to me, not her. Don't...don't hurt her."

Amara looked amused. "I thought she was your brother's bride," she said patronizingly. "But she is a pretty thing, isn't she. I could see her turning your head."

She didn't know about the misplaced mate spell. Of course not, it wasn't something that anyone back home would want to advertise. It was possible that she didn't know about mates at all. "Promise me you won't hurt her," Tray insisted.

He wasn't sure how Amara could manage to look so innocent and so cruel, all at once. "But your highness, you swore it didn't hurt."

"Don't do this to her," Tray said, more desperately now. "Promise me."

"I am a reasonable woman," Amara said. "If I can get from you what I need, I will not need to do the same to her. For now, I commend your desire to protect her." It wasn't exactly a promise.

Tray tried abruptly to twist free, and succeeded in getting one arm free, the arm with the ring. He could feel it slip as he flung himself suddenly forward over the computer desk towards Mackenzie.

The guards were on him at once, grappling him as the computer equipment rattled and Mackenzie backed away in alarm. One of the monitors fell over and a pile of papers fluttered to the floor. He had just enough time to slip the ring into a shallow bowl of computer-related hardware, hoping that it would be disguised with the shining wire clamps and miscellaneous connectors that filled it to overflowing and not slip too far towards the bottom.

Then he was being dragged away in earnest.

17

Leinani paced the room, understanding why caged animals sometimes did this. She was too full of prickling, restless energy to sit quietly and pretend she wasn't worried.

Distance did make her connection with Tray a little weaker, but not so weak that she couldn't feel what they did to him.

Leinani's dragon was suddenly, alarmingly, terrified, and that shook Leinani to her toes. Her dragon was always the steady one, the sure-footed and certain, unbothered by silly human worries and concerns. Until now.

It was hard to describe the sensation, it felt like being peeled from the inside. It wasn't pain, not like the trap they'd been caught in had been. It was like being drained.

They steal! They violate! There was an underlying mix of rage and fear, stronger than anything that Leinani had ever felt from her dragon. *Gone! He's gone!*

Leinani caught herself gasping for air and fought to keep her breathing even. Were they *suffocating* Tray? Were they *killing* him? He wasn't in pain, but the suffering was unmistakable. Waterboarding? she guessed, but it felt as wrong as any other guess she might have.

Her bare feet took her to the door, and she struggled against the spell as long as she could bear it, yearning to go to him, to rage down the hallway in her dragon form and drag her mate back to her side by force.

Not our mate, Leinani protested her dragon's instincts out of habit. *Not ours.*

But there was nothing she could do against the web of magic around the room, or the jeweled collar at her neck. She tugged off her listening ring, but it lay still in her hand and holding it to her ear revealed nothing. Tray must not have been able to set it before…whatever was happening to him had started.

She was pacing again, slipping the ring back on, and she made herself sit, first on the couch, and then at the desk because the chair there had arms that she could clutch at. She used every tool and trick she'd ever learned to try to control her breathing and slow her heart rate, and she still found herself panting on the brink of panic.

She knew by their connection when the guards were bringing Tray back, and was waiting anxiously at the door.

He didn't appear to be hurt, but he did seem stunned, and when the guards pushed him in and the spell activated with a sizzle behind him, he staggered and then simply stood in the entryway for a long moment. The guards didn't bother to shut the door, only left, laughing as they went.

"Tray?" Leinani said softly, coming to stand close to him, but not too close.

He looked at her from very, very far away, not really seeming to recognize her.

"Did they hurt you?" she asked.

He shook his head slowly. "No, I'm not hurt." He

looked down at himself as if to make sure. His shirt was unbuttoned, and it was ridiculously distracting to get glimpses of his skin. "I might have lost some chest hair," he said, with a dull echo of his usual chuckle.

Leinani was sorely tempted to inspect him for injury personally, but she knew that she shouldn't. "What happened? What did they do to you?" She shut the door, letting momentum take it the final few inches so the spell wouldn't shock her.

"They...took him." Tray made no effort to button up his shirt again, just stood, arms dangling loosely at his side. "Amara took...my dragon."

Leinani's breath sucked in. She had guessed as much, but it seemed so impossible that she'd been waiting hopefully for a different answer. *Any* different answer. "How could they do that?"

Tray shook his head, and ran fingers through his hair, making it obvious that he was due for a haircut, as well as getting ridiculously scruffy. "I don't know," he moaned, turning away to gaze out the window. "I don't know. They had a spell, another one of those one-timers, just a piece of paper, and it just...it was like having my teeth pulled out with plenty of novocaine. It didn't hurt, it just...pulled."

"If it's a spell, it will fade," Leinani said firmly, wishing that she dared to touch him. It wasn't just that she wanted him, it was that she wanted to comfort him, and she was afraid that whatever she started, she'd never stop.

Tray made a noise of frustration and grief that nearly upset her resolve. "Come and sit on the couch and have a cup of the terrible tea," she said, reaching for his sleeve and giving the slightest tug.

The couch was still covered in the crumpled blankets he'd slept in, and when Leinani sat and pulled Tray, unresisting, to sit beside her, she was almost overwhelmed by the desire to fold herself into them and inhale. Instead, she stood up quickly, releasing Tray's sleeve, and went to turn on the tiny coffee pot to heat water.

Tray was trying to fasten his shirt when she returned with a cup of sweetened tea, confused by the fact that it was missing a button. "I'm sorry," he said miserably. "I'm so sorry."

"There's nothing to apologize for," she said, sounding prim even to her own ears. "Tray, this isn't your fault."

"If I hadn't followed you, taken you to the trap…"

"Who even knows what would have happened," Leinani scolded him. "I might have been captured on my own. Maybe one of your other brothers would have followed me. Don't borrow trouble from things that might have been." So many things that might have been, she thought wistfully.

Tray gave a sigh, giving up on his shirt. "Might have been," he echoed mournfully. He dropped his head into his hands. "Lights, it's *weird* in here. Hollow."

"Here, drink this," Leinani insisted, daring to sit beside him.

Tray took the cup from her carefully. The biggest benefit to sitting beside him was that it was harder for them to stare at each other accidentally. "Thanks," he said.

"Do you want one of the protein bars?" she offered, feeling helpless. "Are you cold?" Humans were often too cold or hot; it seemed inconvenient.

"No, Mom, I'm fine," Tray said with a dry chuckle. He took a sip of the tea. "This stuff is really nasty."

"Hotel Hovel's finest," Leinani said, folding her hands in her lap so she wouldn't be tempted to sling an arm around Tray to comfort him. "I think they extended the tea leaves with dead bugs. To be honest, I'm not sure it contains *any* actual tea leaves."

Then she startled so violently that Tray nearly fumbled his tea, hot liquid splashing out over his hand. "Ouch!" he said in alarm, not used to that kind of discomfort. "What's wrong?"

It took Leinani a moment to realize that the jolt of alarm running through her was coming from her hand. "My ring!" she said. "You got the other one set?"

"Not well," Tray said mournfully, putting his tea down and sucking on a scalded finger in wonder. "What's it doing?"

"It's...sort of shocking me." Leinani slipped it from her finger and set the ring near her ear, switching sides when it occurred to her that Tray might be able to hear it, too if it was between them. They leaned close together and Leinani realized that she'd made a terrible tactical decision because she could actually feel the heat of him, not quite touching him, and even that set her entire traitorous body on fire.

He knows it, too, she thought in chagrin.

Then the voices started.

Tray sighed in disappointment. "They aren't speaking English."

"Wait," Leinani cautioned him. "The rings should translate, but it might take a moment."

"Impressive," Tray murmured, but quietly, because the voices were coming into focus.

"...But you said that it worked?" a man's voice said dubiously. It might have been the guard that Tray called Scoff.

"It worked," Amara answered. "The dagger was able to act as a conduit and keep the test spell running much longer than we expected. But the power will fade when the dragon returns."

"You got his demon out from him," maybe-Scoff said,

sounding confused. "He was weak, when we took him back to his room. He definitely wasn't a dragon anymore."

Leinani couldn't help herself, and she put the hand not holding the ring on Tray's knee and squeezed. He gave a slight exhale and she took her hand back.

Amara continued, her voice warm. "There are two kinds of magic. Cast magic, and innate."

"Dragons." He said the word with hatred.

"All shifters, to some extent," Amara agreed, her voice silky. "But dragons most of all. Imagine two sheets of flexible plastic, hanging just apart from each other: one magic, and one mundane. At one time, they were close together, touching, and everyone could have access to the power, equally. The shifters came from greedy men who wanted to hoard the magic, who wanted it only for themselves. They separated these worlds, and made themselves the only bridge. We're trying to take that bridge back."

"And our casters?"

"They don't have direct contact with this other world. What they get is like a static shock, or a strike of lightning, here and gone. We deserve better. We deserve *equality*. You, you deserve to be as powerful as they are."

There was a curious sound that puzzled Leinani until the man gave a strangled groan of pleasure and Leinani blushed and almost dropped the ring.

Amara's voice continued after a moment. "This spell will fade. We haven't severed the bond, only borrowed it for a time. But we know it works now, we can do it again."

"Yes, Amara," he growled.

"Now that we know what this spell does, we can set the school to making something better. Something more permanent."

"Yes, Amara... Yes..."

There was a slurping sound that turned Leinani's stomach and the ring went mute, and cool again.

Leinani gave it a little shake, but there was no more sound from it.

"Oh man, it's like when the wifi cuts out right as the good parts in a porno start," Tray said drolly.

Leinani slipped the ring back onto her finger, grateful that he could still joke, even if he sounded—and felt— strained. He didn't even feel as relentlessly horny as he had, something that Leinani had never guessed she would miss.

18

Despite the late hour, Tray didn't feel like sleeping. Leinani made one faint attempt to get him to take the bed and rest, then persuaded him to play the version of Parcheesi that they'd made up around what they understood of the rules and what was left of the pieces. It was a lengthy, complicated affair, and Tray played badly, even by their current standards.

Leinani, trying gamely, kept up a cheery conversation and plied him with terrible tea and snacks that he dutifully ate.

He could feel her worry, but it felt distant, like he was still numb. It bothered him that he missed the immediacy of her feelings more than his own. The pull to her wasn't gone, but it was considerably less strong. And wasn't that what he wanted? To be free of the spell that had mistakenly attached them?

But he didn't actually want to be free of her, and that disturbed him almost as much as the gaping hole in his head where his dragon had always been.

When dawn started to color the mountains, Leinani gave up on the game. "You should try to sleep," she insisted, in that quiet but immovable way that she had.

"I'm not taking the bed," he answered stubbornly.

"Fine," Leinani said, and she stood and shook out his blanket on the couch.

Tray refused to lie down, somehow feeling that if he slept, he might miss his dragon's return, and when Leinani wrapped the blanket around him, he caught her hand and pulled her down beside him.

For a moment, she sat stiffly, then leaned the slightest amount into him. Tray wondered if she was trying to pour her comfort into him deliberately; it felt like a hug that she didn't dare give him physically.

They sat that way for some time, until he felt her soften in his mind...and fall asleep.

He stayed more still than he wanted to, unwilling to disturb the momentary comfort that they had merely to ease his muscles, and watched the light outside the window gradually lighten.

It didn't actually hurt, he realized. But it felt like it ought to, like the emptiness ought to come with some kind of physical affliction.

His dragon's return was gradual and agonizingly slow. At first, it was just a tickle in his mind, like hearing a far-off tap drip; he wasn't sure he actually felt it at all. Then it was a whisper, a familiar brush...but so far away. He had to remind himself to breathe; between Leinani's weight at his side and his intense listening for his dragon, he kept forgetting that he needed air.

You're back, he said in painful relief. *You're back*. Hot tears stung at his dry eyes.

By the time the sun was high, his dragon was swirling in all the corners of his mind that he ought to be, as angry and unsettled by their separation as Tray himself was.

Leinani came awake with an unladylike snort as she started to fall into his lap. "Oh, I'm so sorry," she said, pushing back away from him as soon as she realized where she was. Then she paused, sitting an arm's length down the couch. "Are you…?"

"He's back," Tray assured her. Saying it out loud made it feel real again and he nearly clasped her up in his arms at the joy that she was reflecting back at him.

"I'm so glad!" Leinani said, and the tears that he'd never shed gathered in her eyes. "I'm so glad."

"Don't get all weepy," he said more harshly than he intended. "She's going to do it again."

But not to Leinani she wouldn't, he vowed.

"Hopefully it will take her a while to get a new spell," Leinani said, with her quiet resolve. "She said that the guard should *test* you."

"Strength, I'm guessing? I don't know how else they would know."

"Magic, maybe?" Leinani said.

"Amara's magic isn't like anything I've seen," Tray said in frustration. "Raval, my brother, his magic is like ritual, it's complicated, it's etched in metal for multiple uses, not handwritten like these are. I've never heard of anyone doing it like this, it's such a waste of time and effort. He's always saying that there aren't shortcuts, that it can't be rushed or pressured. But this seems *all* rushed and pressured."

Leinani turned the listening ring that remained on her finger and Tray realized how often he'd seen her playing with them and never thought of them as important. "Those certainly seems useful," he said curiously, wondering if she'd ever intended to tell him about it.

Leinani flushed, perhaps guessing the train of his thought. "They've been in my family since the time of the Compact. My mother gave them to me when Fask first offered for my hand," she said, slipping it off to give it to him. "As someone going far away to be the queen of a very strange place, she thought it might give me an advantage. Not that I intended to eavesdrop on state affairs," she hastened to add. "But it's the kind of thing you can leave on your dresser, to get a sense of what the staff feels about you, or whether there are enemies in the palace."

"You have no enemies in Alaska," Tray hastened to assure her, before he remembered that she'd been kidnapped right out of the country. He held his hand so that she could drop the ring into it without touching him and turned it in the light. It was covered all over with minuscule writing. French? Something older? He wasn't sure. Tray looked through the ring, and put it to his ear. "So, it's not active all the time?"

"It's supposed to be activated by importance," Leinani explained. "You wouldn't want to have to wade through hours of irrelevant gossip. And it translates, of course."

"See, that's what magic should be. Elegant. Classy. Useful. Something that can be used more than once. Something super specific. Did I tell you that one of the spells they used the last time they broke into the castle turned a perfectly good armchair into blue shag? It basically sprouted fur. Why would you even write a spell like that?"

"Was it a mistake?" Leinani theorized. "An error in the activation? Or in the casting itself?"

"It burned away, so we'll probably never know."

Leinani took the ring back, slipping it onto her finger. Tray had to look anywhere else so he wasn't staring at the garish diamond that Fask had given her. "Amara must have a whole army of casters, to be so wasteful with her spells."

"We'll get out, somehow," Tray promised. "We'll get out and we'll stop her."

19

Leinani was very good at talking about nothing. She'd had tutors in the *conversational arts*, as her mother liked to call it, and she had practiced reading people so that she could make them comfortable and draw them out. She could speak intelligently about the weather, fashion, entertainment, and music. She was even skilled at keeping political topics from being contentious.

The problem with talking about nothing with Tray, she swiftly realized, is that it never *stayed* nothing.

"What do you think the weather is like near your home right now?" she asked, when the quiet a few days later was too much to bear. Weather was the safest kind of topic. "Cold, I'd imagine?" She knew she sounded inane...and it bothered her that Tray might think she was shallow. Even more, it bothered her that it bothered her.

"Well, we usually have a few feet of snow by now," Tray said.

They were lying on the floor with their heads close together. She had her feet on a chair, he had his on the couch and was tossing a crumpled wrapper in the air above him. They'd found this was the best way to talk, because there was no temptation to stare at each other, and they could speak quietly, rather than shouting across the room.

She didn't want to admit how much she liked being so close to him, feeling so safe.

"It's usually January that's really cold," Tray continued. "Sometimes we'll get a few weeks of twenty or thirty below."

"It sounds insane," Leinani said, shaking her head. "What do you even do?"

"It's invigorating," Tray said. "Best weather to go out in. Though snow machines don't like it quite that cold."

"I can't imagine anything liking it that cold," Leinani said.

"Dogs do! We go out to about thirty below, and they are always happy to."

"Isn't it cruel?"

"Mushing? Not even a little. Those dogs love to run, nothing in the world makes them happier. They're built for it, and full of energy. My dad used to take me out when I was a kid. Rian always wanted to stay home with his nose in a book, but I loved the trail. The forest is quiet, you know. Maybe you've seen race footage of the dogs barking, but that's only when they're waiting to go, when they're ready and you aren't. When you're running dogs on a deserted trail, it's completely silent out there. You hear every creak of the skis on snow, every pant of the dogs; it's nothing like a snow machine or a car. It's you, your dogs, the whole wild world in front of you."

"Do you do it much?"

Tray shook his head. "Not sledding. My dad used to race a lot, but none of us really picked up the sport. We have one team left, but I mostly take them out two at a time, skijoring."

"What's skijoring?"

"It's like mushing, but you're the sled. Skiing, but hauled along by thirty or sixty pounds of pure energy."

Leinani was quiet for a moment, trying to figure out how to ask. "What happened, with your father? I know what the news says, that he's been ill for a long time now, but no one really knows."

Tray was quiet nearly as long, catching his wrapper and holding it still. "He's asleep. He's been asleep a really long time, now. Rian still thinks he might just come around, but Fask says it's the kind of sleep a dragon his age simply never wakes up from, that there's nothing left of Father inside. We don't know. But I guess the fact that the Compact called a mate for *three* of his heirs indicates that it knows something we don't. Kind of overkill, if you ask me."

Leinani tried to imagine losing her own kind and pragmatic father in such a fashion, the worst of it not knowing whether he lived or not.

"What about Kenth?" she asked. "Speaking of things you don't talk about."

"He and Fask...had a falling out about six years ago now. No one really knows what it was about, but Kenth left and never came back. Rian thought it involved a woman they both liked, but Fask hasn't exactly volunteered any information."

They were both quiet, trying not to think about brothers who wanted the same woman.

"So, what's the weather like in Mo'orea right now?" Tray asked, with his usual determined cheer as he resumed batting his makeshift ball into the air over his head. "Probably not thirty below."

Leinani chuckled. "Hardly. It would be in the eighties during the day, seventies at night. Partly cloudy, a few gentle rainstorms during the week. And our forests are never quiet. There are always a million frogs and insects and birds and geckos trying to loudly win their mates."

"Oh, is that how they do it where you're from?" Tray asked drolly. "I would just stick to a wall and yell at you?"

"With variable levels of success," Leinani giggled.

"Anyway, you probably wouldn't be out dog sledding," Tray observed.

"Surfing," Leinani said wistfully. "Or just swimming. It's mid-afternoon—well, here. The mornings are the best for being out on the water, so I might fly up into the mountains and go cliff diving. Dinner on the beach, if it's nice. We're just past the dry season, now, so it might rain."

"Mmm, dinner," Tray said. "Hot dogs and watermelon?"

"Do I look American to you?" Leinani scoffed. "We'd have fe'i in coconut cream with onions, and chicken roasted in an underground pit. And so much fresh fruit. They warned me that Alaskans would only have one kind of banana, you philistines."

"There's more than one kind of banana?" Tray was so surprised that he missed his wrapper-ball and it smacked him in the face. It rolled to within Leinani's reach and she extended her arm without thinking that maybe she shouldn't; their hands nearly collided.

"So many kinds," she said, snatching her hand back. "Fe'i. Apple bananas. Ice cream bananas."

"Now I know you're pulling my leg," Tray said, retrieving his ball while they pretended that the moment hadn't set them both on fire.

"I'm serious!" Leinani insisted. "Fe'i are a Polynesian orange banana that isn't sweet at all. It's more like plantain, we mostly eat it savory, roasted and smothered in coconut cream. Ice cream bananas are sort of soft and fat and taste a little like vanilla. They have bluish peels. But apple bananas are my favorite; we imported some cultivars from Hawai'i. They are firmer than most commercial bananas, with this delicious green apple tang. They're tiny, too, the perfect little snack." Her stomach rumbled at the reminder.

"Uh, oh," Tray said, drawing away in mock fear. "You woke the beast."

Leinani clutched at her stomach. "Run for your life!" she cried. "It's too late for me!"

Their laughter faded to companionable silence. One of the things that Leinani liked best about Tray was that, as much of a ham as he could be, he didn't feel obligated to fill every silence. It could have been awful, trapped in a room with a man she wasn't supposed to want, if he was also the kind of person who never shut up.

She reminded herself firmly that she wasn't supposed to do anything more than just like him.

They were friends. No-touch friends. And that was working just fine.

There was a knock at the door, and they both scrambled to their feet, carefully staying away from each other. Tray's granola wrapper ball went skidding across the floor, forgotten.

Were they coming to take Tray's dragon away again? Leinani just stopped herself from stepping in front of him defensively. It wasn't the time of day for a meal, despite the fact that talking about bananas had given her an appetite. Once just enough time had passed that they were sure whoever was there wasn't planning to barge in uninvited, as they could at any time, Leinani called graciously, "Come in."

She made herself stand still, folding her hands serenely.

The older maybe-Russian housekeeper was carrying a medium-sized cardboard box. She explained its contents in a rush of foreign speech, then shrugged and shook her head, putting it down on the desk. The guards behind her barely bothered to come in the room, and as quick as they'd come, they were gone.

"Dibs on the box," Tray said swiftly, rounding the couch to collect it.

"What are you, a cat? What are you going to do with a box?"

"You see a box, I see a fort. Or a boat. Or a robot costume."

"It's official," Leinani said. "You've finally cracked." She could barely contain her excitement as he brought it around to the coffee table.

Every day they bundled up their trash and left it at the desk with the dirty towels or sheets. There had been a small pad of paper and a pen in the Scrabble game, so Leinani wrote a short diplomatic note each time with a few simple and specific requests—a kind of food, a sewing kit, music, a pack of cards—and a sincere thank you. She had gotten an apple that way, though it had been a very sad and bruised apple. Tray had insisted that she eat the entire thing. They had eventually been brought another change of clothing, and shoes that were a better fit for her.

It struck her that whatever else she had to take from this whole unwelcome adventure, she had certainly come to appreciate the steady stream of material goods that she had always taken for granted.

Tray opened the flaps and Leinani forced herself not to crowd too close to see. "What is it? What is it??"

It looked like clothing, at a glance, and Leinani would never have imagined she could be this excited for poorly-fitted, second-hand clothing. But when Tray lifted the folded t-shirt on top, he immediately put it back down and grinned at her. "Oh, ambrosia," he said rapturously. "You aren't going to believe it."

"If you don't show me, I'm going to come over there and knock you down," Leinani promised, even though they both knew it was an empty threat.

He looked like he wanted to tease her a little, but ultimately decided not to, flipping the box open in joy. "Books!" he exclaimed. "And if you ever tell Rian I said it that way, I will never speak to you again."

There were half a dozen books inside the box, all of them ragged, well-read paperbacks. Leinani had to hold herself back from reaching in with him to pull them out. "This one is for you," Tray said, holding up one with a shirtless, windswept man standing on the cover.

"Thank you," Leinani said primly, snatching it away from him without touching his hands. She wondered if she would dare to read it. Maybe while Tray was sleeping. It was beginning to feel normal to be at a constant hum of desire. Perhaps the book wouldn't even matter.

The rest were mysteries and thrillers, but beneath them was more treasure.

"A radio!"

"Nope," Tray said, lifting it out. "A cassette tape player!"

Their captors had apparently not trusted them with information from the outside world, but the tiny boom box came with a dozen cartridges in cases, some of them unlabeled. "I've never used one before," Leinani confessed.

"One of Raval's precious old cars has a cassette deck," Tray said. "I bet I can figure it out."

While he found an outlet to test it in, Leinani dove into the box. There was one final item in the bottom with the tapes, about the same size, and she pulled it out and opened it.

"A sewing kit!" she exclaimed in joy. "You can finally fix that hole in your sock, and your missing button, look there are spares. It's even got tiny scissors!"

Tray, after a few false starts, got the tray in the tape player shut and pressed play.

After days—Leinani wasn't even sure how many at this point—of unnatural quiet, the music was almost overwhelming. It was so *normal* that it was jarring, a sudden, shocking reminder of how strange and surreal their life had become.

"Don't cry," Tray begged, before Leinani even realized that she was going to. "Please don't cry. If you cry, I'll cry, and I am way too manly to be okay with that."

Leinani took a few steadying breaths. "I promise," she said.

"Pinky promise?" Tray asked, raising an eyebrow.

"Distance pinky promise," Leinani said, raising her hand with her smallest finger crooked as he did the same. "It's so weird," she said, voice more shaky than she wished it was. "I didn't think it would matter that much."

The tape was an 80's band, Journey, the songs familiar from any classic rock radio station, and it filled the little room with a brightness that Leinani hadn't realized was missing. She rifled through the rest of the cassettes to distract herself. Some of them were unlabeled mixed tapes, there was a collection of easy-listening classical music, and several albums that Leinani shook her head over. "New Kids on the Block?" she said skeptically.

"You could file a complaint," Tray said with a shrug.

"I wouldn't want to seem ungrateful," Leinani conceded.

They listened to four of the tapes that afternoon, and

talked about the songs that they missed most, concerts they had attended, music that they studied.

"I took a few years of flute and eight years of piano," Leinani said. "I am what teachers call technically proficient but uninspired; I'd never make a career of either of them."

Tray, to her surprise, played a little guitar. "Our tutor was actually the one who insisted we each learn an instrument. He said it would teach us math and language more naturally."

"I can see that," Leinani said, thinking about how reading music had always felt a little like trying to read in a foreign language. "Are you good?"

"Nope," Tray said frankly. "I can play the opening of Brown-Eyed Girl and a few measures of Stairway to Heaven, and that's about it."

"We should request a guitar," Leinani suggested. She immediately decided it was a terrible idea, picturing Tray in his rock-star tight pants strumming guitar chords at her.

If he guessed the train of thought that led to her rise of desire, he was kind enough to defuse it by joking, "We could request a piano!"

"Oh yes," Leinani laughed gratefully. "Let's get a baby grand and put it in the conservatory with the pet tiger."

For a moment, she didn't think anything of the buzzing shock on her finger, focused entirely on keeping her thoughts from straying. Then she sat upright on the couch. "My ring!"

Tray's fury blind-sided her and it took her a moment of mental wrestling to realize that he was thinking about her engagement ring, and everything that meant.

"The *listening* ring," she clarified, through clenched teeth, because it made her angry, too. "Just the listening ring."

20

Most of the time, with good concentration, Tray could convince himself that Leinani was just a friend. A really hot, no-touch friend. They had navigated to a perfect balance of distance and closeness to make the isolation bearable, and he could convince himself that safe, platonic fondness was the strongest of his real emotions for her.

But every once in a while, something would remind him that this amazing woman was going to marry his brother and rage and jealousy would swamp him.

He dreaded those moments, knowing that Leinani would pick them up as easily as if he'd said it all out loud, and he hated himself for making it worse for her.

"Sorry," he said tightly as he turned off the tape player. "Sorry."

When she lifted the ring to her ear and beckoned him to sit beside him, he did, still aching as he sat as far from her as he could and still hear.

They had missed some of the conversation.

"—I should know?" Amara was asking.

"This one has the activation word caramel," her assistant said.

"Caramel?" Amara said skeptically.

"Daniel was hungry when he wrote this one. That kind of thing can leak over in very curious ways." Mackenzie paused. "I would like to talk about giving them a little break. We've been going pretty hard with the stone, and we're not really sure what kind of long term effects it might have."

"They are resilient," Amara said dismissively. "And they know what's at stake. Are they actually complaining?"

"No," Mackenzie said reluctantly. "But they wouldn't."

"Of course their best interests are in our heart," Amara said, palpably turning on the charm. "You don't think I'd want to harm them, do you?" She managed to sound hurt.

"No…"

"Have trust, my hand. Our time for victory is near, and we will need all of our warriors ready."

Mackenzie's silence was hard to interpret without visual cues.

"Have the prince brought in. Let's see if we can get the effects to last longer this time. We're more ready this time, we'll do as much as we can with it."

Leinani fumbled the ring in alarm and Tray automatically moved to catch it. Her reflexes were as good as his, and he ended up catching her hand instead of the ring, and then dropping it away at once.

They scrambled apart on the couch and stared at each other, the bond between them swirling in dismay and desire, and Leinani rather suddenly brought the ring to her ear as she remembered it. She slowly lowered it again and shook her head. "They're gone."

Then she looked at the door to their little hotel prison.

"They're coming for you again." Her voice was calm and even; Tray knew very well that she was anything but behind her words.

Have the prince brought in...last longer this time.

If his dragon had possessed a separate body, Tray would have clung to it, remembering the horror of losing him the first time. Clinging to Leinani would have been almost as good, but twice as dangerous.

The only thing he could do was the thing he always did, make a joke of it. "How can we make this more fun?" he asked, getting to his feet. "Maybe if I was naked when they arrived? Nudity is always hilarious. Did you ever hear about the bet I had with my brother? He had to walk around nude for a week when he lost. It was in all the papers. Well, all the *good* papers."

Leinani smiled bravely through the tears that were gathering in her eyes. "Tray…"

"Hey, no crying, you pinky promised."

"Distance pinky promised," she said, blinking hard.

"I'm holding you to that," he said fiercely. "And I'll know if you do."

The noise that they were expecting came then, a cursory knock on the door followed by the click of the keycard and the latch. There were four guards this time, and they had that same all-business air that they'd had last time they had come to collect him. "Sorry to interrupt, your highnesses. Amara requests an audience with the prince." One of them gave a mocking bow.

"Tray…" Leinani started.

"My brain is watching you," he warned, trying to smile through the dread they were both feeling.

Then he vaulted easily over the back of the couch. "Well, gentlemen, let's get this over with."

If they were surprised by his readiness to go, they

didn't betray it on their faces and they fell into step behind him as the room detainment spell flexed and let him through. He desperately hoped that the distance would spare Leinani from the worst of it.

Amara looked pleased to see him, and she wasted no time once he was buckled in. "Remove his shirt."

He was wearing a t-shirt, and the guards argued a moment over whether to unbuckle his restraints to get it off him before Amara handed one of them a pair of scissors with a sigh.

"Hey!" Tray protested as they cut it off. "That's one of the only shirts I actually like! You know, we really could use a wider selection of clothing, if you're taking requests. And we've put in a couple of applications for more games. Maybe a game with all the pieces this time? Did you know that our Scrabble game has no U's? The Q is almost a complete dud. It's like getting the Old Maid. Oh, and a razor. I'm starting to look like a hobo. A really handsome hobo, mind you."

"I'm reconsidering that suggestion to gag him," Amara said with an amused smile.

Tray smiled at her as winningly as he could, not hoping to actually charm her, but desperate to distract himself—and Leinani–from what he knew would come next. "I feel like Captain Kirk," he said lazily. "Ends every episode with a ripped-up shirt. Gets all the girls."

Mackenzie was bringing Amara a small stack of papers and she got very flustered when Tray winked at her.

"You think we'll be able to try all of these before we lose his dragon?" Amara said, looking through the pages curiously.

"It should last considerably longer than last time," Mackenzie assured her.

Tray resisted the urge to struggle against his bonds. If

they were doing this to him, they weren't doing it to Leinani.

At the reminder, he thought he felt her, like a flutter inside his ribcage. He had to be strong and brave, because Leinani would suffer everything he let himself feel.

You'll be back soon, he told his dragon, and neither of them was as confident about it as he wished they were.

Amara took up the topmost paper, looked at Mackenzie, and at her nod, pressed the page to Tray's chest and said, "Caramel."

It would have been absurd if it hadn't been so awful, like he was the bottom of a milkshake being sucked up through a straw. All that was left at the end was a sticky glass.

Amara looked at the dagger in her hand, her face split with joy. "Bring me the first spell!" she commanded.

Mackenzie handed her a page covered in tiny blue printing. "You've used one like this before, but it should be far stronger with the dragon's magic behind it, and it won't fade as soon," she said. "The key is putting the page over the afflicted part and tapping it twice."

"No words?"

Mackenzie shook her head. "Not necessary with this one."

Tray watched with all his concentration, because it meant he wasn't thinking about the agonizing emptiness in his head.

Amara unwound the bandages from her hand and wrapped the paper around the fascinating stumps of her missing fingers, tapping them twice.

The paper burst into flame, but to everyone's surprise and Amara's delight, it didn't simply burn immediately away, but curved into a living shape around Amara's hand, twisting and writhing, tighter and tighter until it was entirely encased in flame. Out of the inferno, which seemed to cause the woman no pain, the stubs of her fingers lengthened and filled out, and when the fire finally went out, her hand was whole.

Amara clutched at it and gave a noise of joy and triumph. "Yes! Yes! Give me another!"

Mackenzie took another page. "Here's one you've used," she said, glancing over it. "The keyword is *convince*. It will be line-of-sight, now, rather than distance."

Amara grabbed the paper in her newly-healed hand. "Convince!" The paper burst into violet flame.

Tray stared at her in amazement and the guards at either side of him sank to their knees.

She was still Amara, but taller, more beautiful, more powerful. She was the kind of woman that kings would kneel to, Tray found himself thinking. She was wise and wonderful, like something out of legend. She was a maker of legend, she could be nothing but right about all things.

Her elation was like a salve over Tray's dragonless soul. Surely even that was a small price to pay simply to be in her presence. He had to help her, swear himself to her...

"Another!" she cried, putting the flaming paper down on the desk, where it showed no signs of going out or lighting anything else on fire.

"This one is a weapon," Mackenzie offered, looking hesitant. Was it possible that she did not worship this woman as Tray himself did? "It will cause an explosion, there is not enough space here to test it. Ah, here, a spell for causing something to grow quickly."

A sad looking house plant was brought from the windowsill and put before Amara. At Mackenzie's direction, Amara stroked the leaves and said "*Atell.*"

The plant shivered, then seemed to explode in all directions with unfurling new growth. Tiny buds shot out from every green branch, and there was a riot of new leaves and tiny white flowers. It kept going, new green branches striking out across the desk, around the monitors, as flowers lost petals and burst into seed and new buds took their place.

"*Shan* will stop it!" Mackenzie called, backing away from the crazy growth as it spilled off the desk. "The command has to come from the same person who set it!"

Amara laughed in joy, letting it go another moment before she halted its expansion with the command.

She was magnificent; she was the most beautiful, powerful thing that Tray had ever seen.

And now her attention was entirely on him.

"How long will this last?" she wanted to know, looking at Tray. He desperately hoped that what she saw would please her.

"A few hours," Mackenzie said. "At the most."

Amara looked disappointed. "A few hours. I expected better."

Mackenzie looked annoyed and Tray was astonished that she was able to feel anything but awe. Then she moved between Tray and the desk, blocking his sight, not of Amara, but of the flaming spell.

He was still gazing, besotted, at Amara when it happened, and although her looks didn't change in the slightest, the lines of her face that Tray had moments ago thought were the most beautiful things in the world were suddenly only cruel. Tray was horrified and disgusted that he'd ever wanted to help her.

He kept his expression schooled; the last week with Leinani had taught him a great deal about control, and he hoped that he was convincing as he smiled dazedly at her.

21

Leinani met Tray at the door and remembered at the last minute that she couldn't pull him into her arms, not least of all because he wasn't wearing a shirt. She glared at the guards until they left, closing the door behind them, and backed into the room ahead of the prince.

"I made tea," she said quietly, leading him around the couch. "And put on one of the unlabeled mixtapes." He sat down in the chair and put his feet on the coffee table.

"It wasn't as bad this time," he reported, but Leinani could feel how untrue it was.

"You know that I can tell how awful it was," she reminded him as she gave him his terrible tea.

When she expected a quick-witted joke, he only sighed. "They tested using my dragon with some spells. They last longer, they're stronger."

"What kind of spells?" Leinani wanted to know, not quite sure what to make of his unease; there was something that he didn't want to tell her.

"They turned a houseplant into a small jungle, and

Amara grew back her missing fingers," Tray said. He went on reluctantly, staring down at the cup of tea in his hands like he wasn't sure when he'd taken it, "And she cast this...glamor, a compulsion. It was like Stockholm syndrome dialed up to eleven. I wanted to help her. I wanted to follow her cause to the ends of the world and throw myself off, if she asked me to."

Leinani absorbed his tangled up feelings, and she thought knew where they came from. "Like...*us?*"

Tray lifted his head from his untasted tea. "No," he said, and Leinani could sense his sincerity. "Nothing like this. You...you're in my head, but you're just...all the things I might feel, all the things you might feel. I get to try to sort it all out into some kind of sense, even if it's sometimes hard because feelings are strong. This was forcing me to feel exactly what she *wanted me* to, I didn't have any choices. No free will." He looked back at his tea. "You're all honesty, whether you want to be or not, and she was all false promises. And it didn't even matter that I knew they were false."

Leinani sat at the end of the couch closest to him and took her own cup of tea. She didn't want tea any more than he did, but it seemed like a nice normal thing to do, a habit from another life. A life that wasn't hers anymore.

"This is all such a mess," she said mournfully. "I keep waiting for it to go away, to wake up, to go back to normal. I don't even know what will seem normal after this."

"We'll never be the same," Tray said, with raw candor. "I mean, we'll probably be okay again, with time and good therapy, but we'll never be exactly who we were again."

Leinani laughed and shook her head. "I feel like me from a week or whenever ago was a completely different person," she agreed. "So naive and sheltered. I didn't even believe that there were people like this in the world, not really. Not outside of stories. I never thought about how *good* my tea was, or how lucky I was to have my freedom. Or a hairbrush, even."

"You're not crying, are you?" Tray said suspiciously. "Because there was a distance pinky promise that I'm totally going to hold you to."

Leinani wasn't sure how Tray, who had just been through so much himself, could possibly make her feel better, but he managed to. "I'm so glad I'm here with you," she said frankly. She quickly added, "I mean, I'm not glad to be here, and I'm not glad that...all this happened. But I'm...glad. That you're here with me."

All of their dangerously warm feelings for each other were laid bare between them, all the gratitude she felt for him echoed back.

"I don't know what I'd do without you," he confessed quietly. "You make everything bearable. I'd be so crazy. I would have given up the second day. I can't imagine a better person to be stuck with."

Leinani didn't have to answer, they both sat and let their appreciation and affection for each other wash over each other for one blissful moment without trying to fight it.

Then the unlabeled mixed tape switched songs and Jessie's Girl came on, lamenting about wanting another guy's girlfriend.

Tray slouched in his chair and put his hand over his forehead. "Okay, universe, I can take a hint, jeez."

Leinani had to laugh, because what else could they really do. "This is a terrible mixtape," she groaned.

"I'll get a shirt," Tray said, rising to his feet and putting his tea down. "I know this much Alaskan prince is just too much to ask you to take, and I'd hate to embarrass you by making you throw yourself at me. I asked for a razor, while

I was there, by the way, but I don't think they were taking requests."

"I think I need one as badly as you do," Leinani confessed. "I have yeti ankles and let's not even talk about *other* areas."

"Wait," Tray said, retracing his steps. "Wait, we can talk about those other areas, if you want. I mean, I'm here to listen. You can lie down on the couch and tell me anything you need to about those bits. I'll take notes."

"Shirt, Tray!" Leinani commanded, covering her flushed face as she pointed to the bedside table he had claimed for his own. "Have mercy!"

The best part was that she knew he was teasing her kindly, that he meant to embarrass her just the right amount, and he would always stop before he went too far.

He gave a show of sighing and pulled a shirt from his drawer. "Seems like a shame to cover all this up, but some people are just ridiculously *prudish.*"

"Yes, prudish is the adjective we'll go with. Drink your tea, prince pink-nipples, and rematch me at Parsnoozy until your dragon returns."

Leinani was setting up the game, complete with altered cards from the Dating Game, when Tray made a strangled noise and his shock and surprise made her turn in alarm. "What's wrong?"

He was standing with his shirt half on, his fingers tangled in the necklace around his neck.

Leinani flinched, expecting a jolt of shared pain that never came.

He clutched at it, eyes wide, and Leinani could feel the alarm and hope coursing through him. "It isn't working," he breathed. "It isn't working."

Leinani got to her feet. "Has the spell faded?" The room spell had been reset twice since they had arrived, the stink of burning paper making the air unpleasant for hours afterwards. Her own fingers strayed toward the choker that no longer felt odd at her throat. She had gotten out of the habit of testing it, disliking the way that it made Tray wince more than the brief discomfort bothered her, and she had quickly learned not to accidentally touch it while dressing or showering. The tiniest brush of her fingers usually brought sizzling torment, and there was a moment of hope this time before she touched the choker and set off the magical restraints.

The anguish felt no less than ever, and Leinani dropped her hand away quickly, even as Tray grasped his in both hands and clawed it off his neck without consequence.

He threw it into the game, scattering the Parcheesi pieces and stood there panting like he'd just run laps of the hotel.

Was it because his necklace was of different construction? Was it less enduring? Or was it because…

"It's because I don't have a dragon," he said in anguish. "The spell is to restrain a *dragon.*"

And he wasn't a dragon anymore. Not for now, at least.

But for now…

"You can get out." Leinani knew that he'd been thinking of it.

Tray walked to the nearest wall and put his hand flat upon it while Leinani watched with her heart in her throat. "Nothing," he reported, and they both looked anxiously at the closed door.

He had to pass her to get to it, and she followed him helplessly.

She could tell how hard it was for him to force himself to try the handle, braced for the agonizing result of every other attempt.

But nothing happened.

The latch turned easily, and the door swung open an inch while they each held their breath. There were, fortunately, no guards directly outside, though they could hear voices further down the hall. Tray went so far as to wave his hand cautiously through the door frame before he closed it again.

Leinani reached her hand out to the latch cautiously. "For science," she quipped, and she touched it for the briefest moment, long enough to know that the spell was still working perfectly on her.

"Don't try that again," Tray begged her, as she staggered back into the room away from the door.

"D-duly noted," Leinani said. "Tray, you can leave," she told him. "You should go, get out, while you can."

"I'm not leaving you here," he said flatly. "You know that."

"You could get help."

"And let them take you somewhere else while I did that? I couldn't shift, I'd have to walk, we don't even know where we are, it might take too long sneaking around to make contact with home. No, we escape together, princess, and I'm not even going to discuss anything else."

"Stop being so stubborn!" Leinani scolded him. "One of us free is better than neither of us! You could at least get them looking for us." Because they weren't, she finally accepted. Everyone still thought that they'd run off together. Even if their families finally went searching, after this long, the trail would be long cold. There was no hope for rescue, there was no hope for escape…panic rose up in her throat.

"No, no, no," Tray said, and he took her by the shoulders for one quick squeeze and then let go. "No crying," he said, gazing hard into her face. "You pinky promised.

Look, we're going to get out, and we're going to get out together. We have a shoehorn now, we know something that they don't. We can use this, but I'm not just going to waltz out and leave you behind, okay? We need a plan, a way to get both of us out."

Leinani wished she could step into his arms and sag against his broad chest for comfort, but she didn't dare. She drew in as deep a breath as she could and nodded miserably. "We'll try," she agreed reluctantly. "But you might have to go alone if we can't figure anything out, and you have to promise me that you will."

Tray looked back at her, jaw set stubbornly.

"Promise me," she said. "Promise."

She wasn't surprised when he wouldn't. She helped him tie the necklace back on—it had snapped in just one place, and it wasn't that noticeable that it was a little tighter now.

22

Time flowed weirdly, and though they joked about scratching tallies in the wall to mark each day, Tray actually wished they had from the beginning, because sometimes it seemed like months had gone by, trapped in the tiny hotel room. Amara continued to drain him of his dragon and test a seemingly endless stream of spells. Sometimes it was only days between their meetings, and sometimes it was so long that Tray began to have thin hope that she'd given up on him for some reason.

In some ways, the hope was worse, because being hauled away to have his dragon stripped from him was always more terrible when it happened.

He and Leinani plotted ways to escape, talking about a future when neither of them had their dragons and they could orchestrate a way out past the spell. They tried practicing self defense moves with each other, but quickly gave that up as a thing that entailed more contact than they dared use. Theory would have to suffice.

Tray's request for a razor continued to go unheeded, though Leinani was at least able to get a supply of feminine necessities that the suspicious probably-Russian housekeeper left with an order of souvlaki and a flat soda that they shared.

"This is...sexist or something," Tray complained, while she was rummaging through the basket for a snack. She seemed past the worst of her embarrassment and he thought it was safe to tease. "Sure, you get the lady sticks you ask for. I'm turning into a chia pet over here and it's damaging my fragile pride. Also, it itches." He was batting a wrapper against the wall with one of the hockey sticks he'd made from a box flap, laboriously cutting it out inch by painful inch with the tiny sewing scissors. He still hadn't gotten around to mending his puppy-chewed sock.

"It's not sexist," Leinani protested in mock-outrage, knowing his joke for what it was. "They just don't want blood all over the furniture. And *lady sticks*? Seriously?"

"You would prefer menstrual mice? Coochie q-tip? Help a guy out."

"Tampons. They are tampons. You need sisters."

Tray was blindsided by the realization: "I do have sisters. Carina now, and Tania, soon enough."

And Leinani.

Because she was marrying Fask. His hands tightened around the cardboard hockey stick and he had to make his fingers relax before he crushed the corrugation.

Most of the time, he could forget it. Her ring was obnoxiously obvious when they were playing board games, but even that had simply faded to just another thing about Leinani that he tried not to think too hard about. Like her gorgeous body, or the way her hair fell around her shoulders, or how kissable her lips always looked.

Other times, like now, he would suddenly, unwelcomely, remember all of it. His dragon, back for the moment, was as convinced as ever that Leinani was meant to be theirs, only theirs.

She lowered her eyes and Tray could feel the whisper of her own frustration and yearning. He grasped for a joke, any joke, but nothing felt funny.

Shouldn't the spell have faded away by now? he wondered. Shouldn't they be free of the future they'd worked so hard to avoid? How many weeks had actually passed? Tray hit the wrapper at the goal again and it bounced behind a chair.

Leinani suddenly clapped her hands. "Wait, wait!" she exclaimed with determined merriment. "If you're going to be my brother, do you know what that means?"

Tray could tell she was trying to help, to distract him from his own dismal thoughts. Most days, they did a good job of dragging each other from despair. "What does it mean?" he asked hopefully.

"I get to be a *little* sister!"

"Aren't you already a little sister?"

Leinani shook her head. "I was a big sister! The oldest, the responsible one. Big sisters have to set examples. Little sisters get to pull pranks and torment their brothers. Big sisters have to protect them."

"Look out," Tray said, slowly smiling.

"I will have my revenge!" Leinani declared.

"Revenge?"

"I came to Alaska when I was a little girl and one of your brothers put a tree frog down my dress. When we get back to Fairbanks, you have to help me get even."

Tray groaned. "About that…"

Leinani's golden eyes got big. "That was you, wasn't it! Oh, I should have known. Who else would it be? Fine, I'll get my revenge on *you*."

"I'll never see it coming," Tray promised with a chuckle.

"What are you afraid of?" Leinani asked. "Spiders? The dark?"

"Chocolate," Tray said, pretending to think about it. "I'm terrified of chocolate."

For one brief moment, she looked confused, undoubtedly thinking about the many chocolate bars they had shared during their imprisonment together.

"And steaks and naps," he added. "Beer. Definitely beer."

Understanding dawned in Leinani's face. "Hockey too, I'm sure."

Tray gave a dramatic shudder. "Not the hockey!" he pleaded.

"My revenge on you will be a hockey game, served with steaks and beer and chocolate," Leinani giggled.

"Followed by a nap," Tray suggested. "Sweet, sweet revenge."

"That sounds wonderful," Leinani said wistfully.

"It will be the first thing I do when we get back," Tray said firmly. "What about you? What are you going to do?"

Leinani looked dreamy. "I want a good meal, and a bed that doesn't sag in the middle, and a shower with shampoo that doesn't leave my hair like straw, and a real hairbrush, followed by tailored clothing." She plucked at the gaping waistband of her jeans. "And I'd like to go flying."

Flying. *Freedom.* Tray let himself indulge in the fantasy a moment.

Even their brief, regretful time together in the sky was a memory that Tray would treasure forever. She was as gorgeous as a dragon as she was a woman, all power and grace. How amazing would it be to tumble through the clouds with her in joyful tandem flight? To leave the earth, and this hateful building, behind…

"Yeah," Leinani said on an exhale.

Tray wondered if she was merely imagining the same thing, or if she was picking up on his own longing. It would have been convenient if the mate spell from the Compact came with nice, neat, obvious end credits. It was like he was stuck in the worst art film ever, and it was never going to end.

"Oh!" she said, with that shiver that Tray recognized now. He put aside the cardboard hockey stick and came to sit beside her on the couch as she lifted the ring so that they could both hear.

Most of the conversations they overheard made no sense without more context, talking about people that they hadn't met, plans that they didn't know the end goals for, but they had started to piece together the fact that the hotel was the base for a cult that spanned the world, convinced that magic was being hoarded by shifters and a demon-ridden royal elite.

Amara, as far as they could tell, was revered, and when she spoke, everyone else fell willingly—even worshipfully—into line. What little they overheard of the rhetoric that she gave to her followers seemed disjointed at best, and complete nonsense at least. Tray suspected that she was using an enchantment spell, after his own encounter. It appeared that she had completely locked the hotel down from the outside world; theirs wasn't the only room that had been stripped of televisions, radios, and telephones, and no one but Amara seemed to have a cellphone.

She was talking to one of the guards now; a new recruit, if Tray guessed correctly, who was asking to call his family.

"Your family wouldn't understand," Amara said

sympathetically. "Contacting them would only put them in danger. The Cause is your family, now."

"Isolate and indoctrinate," Leinani suggested dryly. "If anyone is hoarding magic, it's Amara, with her creepy brainwashed cultists writing her spells."

"I just don't want them to get hurt," the guard said plaintively.

"Would they have the same consideration for you?" Amara asked gently. "You said yourself that they are helpless pawns to the treacherous media. They are lost to sense, fed lies and falsehoods."

"Pot," Tray murmured.

"Meet kettle," Leinani answered, just as low.

"They will see the truth, when we succeed at last," Amara promised. "All who are not destroyed in the flood will rise with it."

"Yes, Amara," the man murmured.

"It will be soon," Amara said seductively. "So soon. At the new year, with the turning of the calendar, we will call the cause together for a glorious campaign. The royals will fall, and the magic will be in the hands of the people again."

"Yes, Amara." He sounded dreamy.

"Go and ready your brothers and sisters," Amara commanded. "Ah, Mackenzie, come in and show me what you have."

23

Leinani knew that the sound of the hotel door lock was going to be one of those things that would cause a spike of anxiety in her chest for the rest of her life.

"Field day for a therapist," Tray muttered *soto voce*, confirming that it did the same thing for him.

They never knew...was this going to be a simple delivery of food or consumables? Some other unexpected fulfillment of their requests, like the cassette tape player and the games? Or were they going to drag Tray off for more experimentation? Leinani had a stab of fear that she wasn't confident was her own. Maybe it was *her* turn at last.

They both stood up from where they'd been lying by the Scrabble game on the floor. Tray was winning handily, again, and they had been debating whether or not they should start preparing a dinner meal from their stash of food as the sunset stained the mountains outside. It was near the time that they would get a food delivery, if they were going to get one, and they were turning over their alternate options. They had a good number of the noodle cups, now, and some protein bars; they never went to bed hungry, though Leinani could not remember the last time she'd been truly *full*.

The smell that came in with the guards was enough to make her stomach growl, and one of them was carrying a steaming platter, heaped high with dishes.

"What's the occasion?" Tray asked, staring as they put it down on the desk and backed out. He sounded more stunned than sarcastic.

"Feliz Navidad!" Snort said with his namesake noise. They had named all of the guards, though every so often a new one would show up and Tray and Leinani would have to argue over what to call them.

The door clicked shut with that same heartstopping sound.

"Christmas?" Leinani said in disbelief. She couldn't decide if she was shocked that it was already Christmas, or dismayed that it was only Christmas. Time in their tiny hotel had shrunk with their confinement. Every day blurred into the next, varied only occasionally by Tray's terrible torture.

"I didn't get you a gift, Princess," Tray said apologetically. He waited for Leinani to go past their little sitting area to the desk; they had gotten very good at sharing the space considerately, and at allowing no opportunity for inadvertent touch.

"I can't believe it's Christmas," Leinani said, with a little catch to her breath that she couldn't quite stifle. Not that she'd have been able to hide her distress from Tray anyway... "We've been here for a *whole month*."

She glanced at him as she brought the heavy tray to the coffee table. The mate spell should have faded by now, and certainly the rough edges were off of their connection. But she thought that it was just that they had effectively reined in their worst impulses, weathered the keenest stage of the mistaken connection, and changed their future. His friendship was of more value now than her unabated desperate desire for him, and his dearness in her heart was more compelling than his perfect body.

He caught her glance and she felt an undeniable twang in her heart. Their connection was not gone. They had just changed it, successfully. Exactly as they intended.

Leinani refused to think about why that somehow made her so sad, and stuffed her feelings aside before he might pick up on them to marvel whole-heartedly over the spread.

There were slices of honeyed ham, fresh rolls, some kind of creamed vegetable casserole topped with crunchy bread crumbs, portions of green salad with an Italian dressing, slices of iced sweet bread, bowls of olives…

"No knives," Tray observed.

"Did you really think that they would give us knives?" Leinani asked.

"I was hoping," Tray said, demonstrating that even Alaskan princes were not above putting olives on all their fingers. "I'm desperate enough to shave with a steak knife."

Leinani served herself a plate of the goodies and settled onto the floor so that they weren't crowding the platter together.

"I didn't even think to miss ham," Tray said, abandoning utensils altogether to eat a slab of it with his fingers —he'd eaten all his olives already. "Oh ham, I will never stray again, my sweet, sweet porcine friend."

"It's still hot," Leinani said in delight. "Oh, there's butter for the rolls."

There was even a knife for the butter, a dull, flat spreading utensil that was utterly no use for escape.

"I am buttering everything," Tray declared, after he jokingly pretended to shave with it. "Even my salad."

"I might cry," Leinani warned him. "There is actual green salad."

"No crying," Tray reminded her. "You distance pinky promised."

"You're right, I'm too busy eating to cry," Leinani corrected merrily. "There are three rolls."

"I will fight you for the sweet bread," Tray threatened. "But I graciously grant you the extra roll."

"We should save it for later," Leinani said reluctantly, and she laughed and shook her head. "To think that a month ago I wouldn't have given a roll a second glance, let alone have hoarded it for the future."

She knew that Tray was looking at her before she looked up. He was chewing, thoughtfully, and Leinani wanted to beg him never to shave.

"I should have gotten you an escape from our prison for Christmas," he said lightly.

"That's just what I always wanted," she answered, just as carefully careless. "But it wouldn't fit in my stocking. Oh, we didn't hang stockings last night. No wonder Santa didn't come."

"My sock still has a hole in it, but I would have left out a pack of those vending machine cookies if I'd known," Tray chuckled.

"I would have given him my engagement ring," Leinani said, only hearing the words after she spoke them. "Because...ah...I only meant that it's the most expensive thing I have."

Tray shot her one of his crooked, heart-felt smiles. "I know," he said.

He wasn't bothered, Leinani realized suddenly. There was no jolt of anger in her head at the idea of her marrying someone else. He'd gotten through the spell exactly as they intended, unscathed, his feelings for her only platonic.

She smiled at him, her best and bravest company smile, and bent to her food before her expression could crumble. She could still feel *him*, aware of his nearness and his solid, reassuring presence. She just didn't feel that keen, brain-eating longing that they'd had for each other from him. With luck he couldn't hear her undimmed passion for him. She wondered suddenly if having her dragon meant the spell dragged on longer for her. Dragons were more sensitive to magic, and he was so often without his now…

"What would you be eating, if you were at home for Christmas?" Tray asked, when they had slowed their consumption enough to converse.

"Fresh fruit," Leinani said longingly. "Pineapples and mangos and bananas, *apple* bananas. And fresh bread. Pies. Platters of cheese and olives all day, with buttery crackers. A glass of good wine, though at this point, a *box* of wine would feel decadent." Tap water had long since lost its objectionable flavor and turned into normalcy. "You?"

"One year, we had reindeer sausages in honor of Rudolph the red-nosed reindeer."

Leinani had been taking a sip of her water at that moment and she struggled to keep it in her mouth. "You didn't!" she exclaimed, once she had stopped coughing.

"Toren's idea, and everyone thought it was hilarious. Mrs. James put pimentos on the ends for red noses. We had casserole with it, and bread, and green salad. Lots of olives and carrot sticks. Pie for dessert, about seven kinds."

"I don't think I've ever had reindeer," Leinani said. "Is it good?"

"Not as gamey as moose," Tray said easily. "It's as good

as beef, very mild, but super lean. You'd probably like it, even with your princess standards."

"My princess standards have become remarkably lax," Leinani said wryly. "I think I ate too much. I can't remember the last time I was this stuffed." She wiped her mouth on one of the linen napkins that had been served with their meal and wistfully remembered when linen napkins had been *normal.*

"I should have Instagrammed that meal," Tray said, leaning back and making a show of unbuttoning his pants. They were still rockstar tight, but he seemed to have gotten used to them.

"You don't have an Instagram," Leinani scoffed.

"I sure do!" Tray insisted. "Like a hundred thousand followers, all of them glued to the food I eat and my gorgeous puppies. You probably have one of those snooty Twitter accounts, where you're all clever and writing haikus in 150 words or whatever. Hashtag, princess."

"280 characters," Leinani giggled. "And I mostly just retweeted stuff by clever people writing the haikus. Hashtag, dork." She sobered suddenly. "Do-do you think anyone misses us?" What had social media made of their sudden disappearance? What story had the two monarchies offered to explain it away? What did her mother and father think? Were her brothers convinced by whatever cover story was being trotted in front of the press?

Had Fask publicly called off the engagement, with no bride at hand for a whole month?

The grief she felt was too keen to be only her own. "I imagine they must be looking for us now," Tray said comfortingly.

"They'll be celebrating Christmas right now," Leinani said, trying to keep her face serene even though her meal was sitting in the bottom of her stomach like a rock. "I...

wonder if they expected us to waltz in at the last minute and take our empty chairs."

Tray laughed dryly. "I can imagine the looks on their faces if we did."

They sat quietly, nibbling on the last crumbs on their plates.

"I...ah...I think I'll take a shower before bed," Leinani finally said.

"I'll clear up," Tray offered, getting gracefully to his feet and bending to wrap their leftovers. Dragon or not, he still moved like an athlete.

Leinani went into the bathroom. She took down the clean clothing hanging in the shower and turned on the water, then sat numbly on the edge of the tub.

It was Christmas.

A Christmas like no Christmas she had ever imagined possible.

She wondered if Tray would know if she let herself cry, or if it still mattered if she held her feelings together on those rare moments when she was alone.

After a dry-eyed moment, she stood and went to the counter, where she unwrapped a tiny hotel soap and smoothed the paper down. Then she smiled, as an idea struck her.

24

The moment Leinani shut the bathroom door behind her, Tray sprang into action.

There was no way that he was going to let her get through Christmas without a present. He ransacked the games, desperate for an idea, and paused at the card from The Dating Game that Leinani had added the hockey stick and stubble to. He smiled at it fondly, rubbing it with his thumb, and tucked it back into the box. Nothing here was a good gift. He rummaged through the drawer in his bedside table and found the socks he'd been wearing when they arrived, the puppy-chewed hole that he'd never gotten around to mending in one toe. The hard-won sewing kit was still sitting on the table and Tray suddenly remembered the mis-matched buttons that had come with it.

By the time he heard Leinani's water turn off, after a conveniently long shower, he had stitched the two remaining buttons to the unmarred sock, and embroidered a few wandering lines in red thread on the dark material.

He hastily wrapped it in one of the cloth napkins that had come with their dinner, and was standing by the bed when she came out of the bathroom, a towel still wrapped tight around her hair in one of those impossible magical turbans. She was holding something cupped in her hands, and she was smiling.

"I made you a Christmas present," she said shyly.

"In the bathroom?"

"It's not that much of a Christmas present, okay?"

"I will love it," Tray promised hastily. "I made you something, too."

They grinned at each other a moment, then carefully exchanged their poorly wrapped gifts.

Hers was tucked almost elegantly in toilet paper, which tore away to reveal a tiny flower, folded from a fresh soap wrapper. "It is the most cunning thing I've ever seen," Tray assured her. "I'll wear it in my hair."

"Beard flowers are a thing," she teased him.

He tried unsuccessfully to anchor it there, and gave up when he didn't want to accidentally crush it. "It's your turn," he reminded her.

She unfolded the napkin and lifted out a sock, turning it in her hands. "Um…"

"It's a sock puppet," he explained. "That's—"

"The tongue!" Leinani exclaimed in delight. She slipped her hand into it and placed her fingers so that she could get the tongue positioned over her thumb correctly. "Om nom nom!" She made bite-y motions in Tray's direction. "Needs teeth," she said. "He'll gum you to death!"

"Is it a he?" Tray wanted to know.

Leinani turned the puppet towards herself and they nodded at each other. "Indeed he is," she giggled. "I think his name is Brett."

"Brett?"

"Brett the Button-eyed, easily the best-looking tenant of room four-seventeen."

"I'm wounded!" Tray said, laughing.

"Are you jealous of a sock puppet?" Leinani teased, petting it.

"So jealous!" Tray meant it as a joke, and he grinned at her, but he could feel the truth behind his words, watching her stroke the sock.

If anything, he wanted her touch more than ever now, craved closeness with her that had little to do with sex or desire. He wanted to be able to smooth her hair back and sit shoulder-to-shoulder with her at the couch without hesitation, to wrestle extra points from her in their cardboard hockey games. He wanted to see where she was ticklish, and feel the solid warmth of her in his arms when she needed comfort.

It was the worst kind of torture, and he felt like his heart might crack, watching her snuggle the puppet into the curve of her neck like a pet.

Yeah. He was jealous of a sock puppet.

If she suspected his thoughts, she didn't give any indication of it; she only looked grateful and playful. Tray turned thoughtfully to look at his reflection out of the window before he lowered the blinds. He couldn't tell anymore, not for sure. He could guess, from her easy smile - there were little tight spots around her eyes that she got when she was trying to be strong, and they weren't there now. But he didn't *know*.

The spell was gone. They'd successfully weathered it.

And he was more in love with her than ever.

She is meant to be ours, his dragon said with confidence.

She was meant for Fask, Tray reminded him. *She was meant to be a queen.*

She will be our queen, his dragon purred.

Tray turned back to look at Leinani and hoped that the catch in his heart didn't show on his face. She was making a space of honor for the puppet on the bedside table. Her hair, still damp, was loose across her shoulders and she was wearing a t-shirt that was too big for her, and she still managed to look like royalty.

She *was* his queen. She was his everything.

And he didn't dare tell her.

It was possible—likely, even—that she'd come out the other side of the spell with nothing more than affection. Tray knew that she liked him, and he suspected that they would always have something of a bond, as much for their shared experiences as the spell that they'd finally shaken off. But she was sensible and strong, and her will was undeniable.

He was jealous again, this time of *her*, for being stronger than he was. When she turned to smile joyfully at him, he could grin convincingly back.

He might be too weak to resist her, but he was never going to tell her so.

25

*L*einani woke leisurely.

Most mornings, worry and fear crowded into her mind at once, and coupled with gnawing hunger, she could not rest even a moment after she realized that she was awake.

But the morning after Christmas felt different. Brett was snuggled up on the pillow next to her, one of his button eyes against her cheek. Her belly was still satisfied by the feast the night before, and she could, for a few moments, think only about Tray's laughter, and his gift, and his happiness as they enjoyed the little luxuries that had once been so common and taken for granted.

Then she remembered that it wasn't exactly *safe* to think about him like that, and she made herself open her eyes.

Tray was already awake, courteously staying quiet as he gazed up at the ceiling. His feet were propped up on the far arm of the couch and Leinani felt guilty that she'd never convinced him to take the bed.

He must have sensed her chagrin, because he turned his head then. "Happy Boxing Day!" he said cheerfully.

"Do you celebrate that in Alaska?" Leinani asked.

"Not except as an excuse to dodge chores and drink beer," Tray chuckled. He sat up, throwing off his blanket. "And eat leftovers, of course."

"We have *leftovers*," Leinani said in delight. She slid out from under her sheets with only slightly less decorum. It felt almost normal to sleep in her clothing now. Between trying to keep her thoughts from straying to sexy places and the fact that they might be disturbed at any time, it was just easier that way.

The food was not quite as good reheated in the little microwave, and there was only one roll between them, but it was still a relative feast, and Leinani was not sure she had been as happy since they had first arrived.

After breakfast and cleaning it up, she took a bath and re-read one of the thrillers. They had both read each of the books several times by now, even the shirtless "man-chest" book, though Leinani had to skip not only the sex scenes but also the confessions of love and concentrate on the underlying action plot—she still wasn't sure if Tray had deliberately read the chapters she had flipped through just to torture her. That had certainly been an awkward afternoon.

They played a game of Scrabble after Tray's shower, ate a lunch of noodle soup (they had spoons now), and sat drinking terrible tea and talking wistfully about holiday traditions with their families in the afternoon. Leinani did a little dutiful yoga while Tray used the cardboard hockey stick to lazily hit a wadded up wrapper at a goal he had drawn on the wall. She had mock-scolded him about being charged damages by the hotel when he drew them.

Dinner was the last of the leftover food, and a granola

bar apiece, once they decided that it was so late that they were unlikely to get a delivery of fresh food.

"This wasn't such a bad day," she said, after she'd finished brushing her teeth. They were getting painfully low on the toothpaste samples, she was barely able to squeeze enough from the packages to taste it now. She had added toothpaste to her recent requests. Her notes weren't as chatty now, as she was getting to the last few pages of the pad that had been in the Scrabble game, and she kept her handwriting as small as it would still be legible. She and Tray didn't write down their scores anymore, in part to conserve the paper, but also to add the challenge of keeping tallies in their head. It made it easier to cheat, but neither of them did, because neither of them really cared whether they won.

"Not a bad day for being locked in a hotel room with my brother's bride and periodically tortured by a madwoman, you mean?" Tray asked drolly. He was idly reading the ingredients on one of the chip bags. "Did you know that these have actual cheese in them?"

"Actual cheese?" Leinani said in exaggerated surprise. "I am agog."

They both stiffened when there was a brief knock at the door and the sound of a keycard before they had time to answer. Leinani glanced out the window to confirm that it was quite late at night; the sun was long down.

The guards who came in were all business, and they carried nothing but guns.

Leinani looked wretchedly at Tray as he stood up in resignation. Throwing herself between them would do no good; there was nothing she could do to protect him and it made her stomach twist. She felt helplessly angry.

"No time off for good behavior, I guess," he said with a shrug. "Happy Boxing Day to me."

"We don't want you, highness," Scoff sneered. "Amara wants the princess."

Tray jerked as if they'd shot him. "No, no, she promised! I have my dragon again, you can take me, you don't get to do this to her."

He had come halfway around the couch, and he stopped where he was, blocking her path out of the room. All of the guns were trained on him and Leinani was suddenly terrified that he was going to do something colossally stupid.

He was strong enough to take a few of them down if he chose to fight, she knew, and they wouldn't want to shoot Amara's magical battery and risk her wrath, but they could use the excuse to hurt him.

"Don't, Tray, I'll go!" she said quickly. Rather than trying to push past him, she clambered over the back of the couch, putting herself between them as she faced him down. "Tray, Tray, don't do anything foolish."

He growled, looking past her at the guards, until she closed the space between them and took his hands, which made him look down at them in shock. "Focus, Tray," she said firmly. "I'll be back. We can't fight yet."

He was still staring at his hands where she was holding them, like he couldn't figure out what she was doing. She let go of one of them and, standing so that the guards couldn't quite see what she was doing, pointed her fingers at her collar. Their chance for escape was together. And the only way that would happen was if they both lost their dragons.

He gazed at her in horror and dismay. "Lei…"

"We don't have much of a choice," she reminded him in a low voice.

"You should listen to your girlfriend," Snort suggested scornfully.

Tray's gaze flickered up over her shoulder with smoldering anger and Leinani realized that she was still holding desperately to his hand. It felt so good in hers, like it belonged there. She wanted to take another step towards him, to close that distance and lean right into him. She settled for giving his hand a final squeeze and stepping back.

One of the guards took her roughly by the arm and pulled her out into the hall, slamming the door behind them.

"Good thing you convinced his highness to lay off," a guard said behind her as they started to march her down the hallway. "We would have put a hurt down on him."

Leinani drew to a stop and turned to stare him down; they were all surprised enough to stop with her and step back. "You are a fool," she said bluntly. "You have no idea what you are dealing with, or how badly you are going to regret your life decisions at the end of this. You should be thanking me for saving you a lot of pain and grief just now." She lifted her chin and rolled her shoulders back. "Now take me to Amara."

26

Tray let Leinani go, knowing and hating that she was right, and immediately threw himself at the closed door behind her, just so that the spell would hurt him and he would feel something that wasn't just helplessness.

It didn't matter if he hurt himself now, because Leinani wouldn't feel it.

Once the burning pain had worn off and he could pick himself up off the floor, he got up and tidied the room, smoothing the comforter on the bed and folding back the corner. He plumped her pillow, pausing to draw it into his arms and inhale. It was so curious and so wrong to have the room to himself, knowing that she wasn't just through the door in the bathroom.

It was ugly-quiet without her, but music was only worse when he tried it.

He played a vicious hockey game with himself, until he realized that he had mangled the cardboard stick past repair. Who even knew when they would get another cardboard box. He threw it across the room and tried to rip the necklace off his neck so he could shift and rampage down the hall to save his mate and destroy everyone who played a role in her harm.

He only succeeded in knocking himself nearly unconscious, and when he could stand up again, he quietly set about getting a cup of tea ready for her return.

He was waiting at the door, and the moment the guards pushed her through, he folded her into his arms without the slightest hesitation. For a moment, she was wooden in his unexpected embrace, then she slowly sagged, weeping, against his chest.

"Shhhh," he said helplessly into her hair. "Shhh, it gets better. It gets better. I'm here, I've got you."

He continued to murmur nothings as he drew her into the room, around the couch to the bed. The guards retreated to the hall and shut the door. It was almost dawn, the horizon just beginning to color the mountains outside the windows.

It was its own kind of torture, having her so close, but Tray couldn't let go, not if hugging her gave her any tiny amount of comfort. She sobbed raggedly, and it broke Tray's heart into pieces to see her so shaken after all of her strength and resilience. He stroked her hair and pulled her down with him onto the bed, curling tight around her while she trembled in shock.

"I know," he said helplessly. "I *know*." He didn't rib her once about her promise not to cry.

She only cried for a few moments, but it was agonizing, and her stillness afterwards only made Tray ache for her more. "I'm sorry," he said, kissing the top of head even as he realized how careful he needed to be. He couldn't protect her from Amara, but he could protect her from himself, keep things strictly platonic, pretend that he didn't still desperately want her.

The spell was gone and none of his feelings had dampened in the slightest. If it could have been called love before, it was something even more now, after spending so much time growing to appreciate Leinani's depth and serenity. She was so brave and beautiful and witty. His enchanted admiration of her had changed, as if it had grown roots and dug in even deeper. He respected her. It wasn't magical, and it wasn't physical...or at least, it wasn't only physical.

Tray started to unwind himself, not sure how long he could keep his carnal need for her from manifesting, and she gave a whimper of protest and clutched at his shirt, holding him close. "Don't go," she begged. "Don't."

Tray drew her closer, willing his body not to betray him. She needed him like this, as a friend. She needed his comfort, and he poured it into her to the best of his ability, cradling her without inviting anything more.

"It gets easier," he assured her. "I'll help you. I'll be here. I'm not going anywhere." His dragon keened in his head, distressed by her suffering.

Slowly, he felt her relax and go limp, and he was just able to keep himself from nuzzling her hair. "I'm sorry," he said quietly. "For all of this. You should sleep, if you can. Your dragon will be back in a few hours."

"I'm too empty to sleep," she murmured, and he squeezed her close in sympathy.

"I could sing you a lullaby," he offered, teasing, "Maybe something in Spanish?"

"I speak French, remember? Not Spanish." But she giggled faintly.

"Perfect," Tray said broadly. "Then you won't know if I'm actually singing a lullaby or a song about hot bikini women drinking out of coconuts."

"I would give my eyeteeth for a coconut," Leinani sighed.

"Can I have the hot bikini women *and* the coconuts?" Tray wanted to know.

She giggled in earnest then, and when she made a tiny movement for freedom, he let her go. It was almost physical pain, releasing her, and he had to set her away quickly or he'd clasp her back.

She didn't go far, simply rolling away until they weren't touching, staring at the ceiling. "Do you think that Amara really can ever...take them away forever?"

"Spells don't last," Tray reminded her. "Not even the biggest and most complicated spells in history. Even the Compact has to be renewed."

Her sideways look was appraising. Was she examining the fact that the mate spell had finally eased for her as well? Was she happily free of the compulsion that had eaten them alive for so long, or had it been replaced as it had been for him, with something more complex and true?

The engagement ring that she still wore glittered accusingly as she sat up and turned her hands gracefully into each other.

Grief, Tray had to guess, gazing up at her, because he received no clues from the dissipated spell or her dispassionate face. She wasn't thinking about him, she was thinking about the dragon that had just been ripped from her soul.

She raised her fingers to her throat and very carefully caressed the choker at her neck. When nothing happened, she sat up and, hands trembling, reached back to release it.

Tray sat up, but didn't offer to help her, even when she fumbled it. He knew how much it would mean to her to remove it herself.

Tears glittered in her eyes but didn't fall as she stared at the choker in her hand and touched her neck in wonder.

"You could—"

"Don't," she hissed. "I'm not leaving without you any more than you would have gone without me."

Tray could not doubt her resolve, and he didn't offer to help her put the choker back on, though it took her several tries to get the clasp back into place.

"Oh!" she said suddenly, startling so suddenly that Tray feared the spell had hurt her. "It's the ring!"

For a moment, Tray could only think of the hated diamond that his brother had given her, then realized that she was slipping off her listening ring. She lay back down beside him with the ring between them so they could both hear.

It was Mackenzie, and she sounded angry.

"You can't drive them like this!" she insisted. "We're starting to see side effects we didn't anticipate! They can't continue to do this!" She sounded on the edge of hysterical.

As always, Amara sounded calm and reasonable. "Mackenzie," she chided, "you know I care for them, very much. I'm not requiring more from them than they want to do. Ask them yourself, they're happy to do this."

"They want to please you," Mackenzie hissed in return. "They are afraid of you and they don't understand their own limits. You're asking too much."

"Afraid?" Amara's voice took on a note of iron. "They know I love them," she said richly. "They know I will do anything for them. I don't ask more than they are willing to do in return. They are a part of a thing that is greater than any of us, and they understand this, as I think perhaps you do not right now."

There was a crash and a loud metallic rattle that made

both Tray and Leinani wince and pull away from the ring. Tray imagined that Mackenzie had slammed her hands down on the desk and made the bowl of hardware shake.

The conversation was less clear after that, and Tray feared that the ring had settled further down into the wire clamps and screws.

"Mackenzie," Amara said chidingly, clear for a moment. "Mackenzie, control yourself! You know we have a greater purpose here. You know that you will be part of making a better world. They know that, too. Come, my hand, listen to your heart. Remember what you're working towards."

The conversation hushed, as if they were walking away from the desk, and Tray realized that he and Leinani were almost touching again, listening close together. She smelled like the hotel soap, and he could still remember the heady scent of tropical flowers that she'd been wearing at Toren and Carina's wedding. Her hair tickled his ear.

The murmur rose again in volume after a short time. Mackenzie sounded abashed. "Yes, of course, Amara. I understand. We'll do our best."

The conversation faded again, and there was the snick of a door closing. "We're losing control of that one," Amara said thoughtfully. "I want you to keep an extra close eye on her."

"Should we restrict her movements?" Scoff wanted to know.

"No," Amara said, her voice already fading with her footsteps away from the desk. "We need her particular talents, and I don't want to spook her. Not yet…"

The ring went quiet and Leinani seemed to realize how close she was lying to Tray. She jolted away and sat up, slipping the ring back onto her finger.

Tray also sat, trying to look casual and nonchalant.

"You really should try to get sleep," he said, swinging his legs off the bed. "It's hard. What you just went through. I know." He yawned and gave an exaggerated stretch. "And the couch is calling me. I waited up all night, you know. That whole platonic worried roommate thing."

"Tray…"

"I'm used to seeing the dawn from this end," he said carelessly, braced against the plaintive note in Leinani's voice. He wouldn't be able to say no if she asked him to stay in the bed with him. "But *you*, Princess, you *really* need your beauty rest."

As he had hoped, her mouth curved into a smile and she chuckled and touched her hair. "That bad?"

"You'd frighten small children," he assured her kindly. "Give them nightmares for weeks."

She rubbed the palm of one hand sheepishly across her cheek, where her brief tears had left tracks. "We wouldn't want that," she said shyly.

"I'll turn off the light for you," Tray said, "and tuck you in as tight as a bug in a rug."

Leinani lay slowly back on the pillows and slipped her legs under the light comforter, looking exhausted as she curled onto her side. Tray pulled the comforter up to her chin and made a show of tucking it carefully around her shoulders. He found Brett and told himself he wasn't jealous that she could snuggle down with a sock puppet.

Her eyes were golden pools of despair, and she looked painfully exhausted as she took Brett and folded him under her chin.

"She'll come back," he promised her. "If you can sleep, she'll be back before you wake."

"Don't go," she whispered as her face crumpled. "Don't go yet."

Her hand grasped towards him under the covers and

Tray covered it with his, glad that the layers between them meant he could clasp it without worrying that he would break his resolve. "You'll be okay," he repeated. "She'll be back bossing you around by about noon and you'll wonder why you ever missed her."

His own dragon knew the joke for what it was and gave a tired swirl of amusement.

Leinani's impossibly long eyelashes fluttered down over her cheeks as she closed her eyes and Tray was glad to watch her gradually relax as he rubbed her hand slowly through the blanket.

"Tell me a story?" she invited quietly. "The story of the bet that had your twin brother walking naked around the castle for a week, maybe?"

"Oh, no," Tray laughed. "That story goes to the grave with me. I'll tell you the story of the time I escaped from Mrs. James and ran away to be a sled dog."

"You mean a musher?" Leinani corrected, opening her eyes.

"No, no," Tray assured her. "I was five, and I was going to be a sled dog. I figured that if I could change into a dragon, it would be even easier to change into a dog, and by the lights, I was going to do it. I couldn't fly yet, but I put on a harness and let dogs off their leads because I hadn't actually thought about how I was going to get us all hooked up to a sled, or what we'd do once I had. It took all night and halfway into the next day before my brothers and I tracked down all the dogs. Fask put me on a leash for the entire search."

"Do you miss them?"

"My dogs?"

She chuckled. "I meant your brothers, but whatever works."

"Well, I miss my *dogs*," Tray said flippantly. "Phoebe

had puppies just about...what month is it, again? The puppies will be weaned by now. Four of the fuzziest little wiggle sausages you ever saw, already chock full of personality. Like furry jello with teeth and attitudes. They probably aren't through the chewing stage, which is rough on mittens and boots...and socks..."

27

Leinani didn't really sleep, but she sank into a safe, comfortable doze, Tray's hand over hers making lazy circles as he talked lovingly about the puppies, describing each one in turn: Moose, an active female dog already claimed by Carina. Tansy, her gentler sister, bonding with Tania. "She's a smart dog," Tray said warmly. "We might be able to train her to be a service dog."

Would Leilani be expected to adopt a puppy as part of joining the Alaska royal family as well? she wondered wistfully. Then she remembered that she would be welcomed to the family as Fask's bride, not Tray's.

She ached, not exactly with physical pain, but with yearning. She wanted to feel Tray's skin against hers, not separated by layers of fabric. She wanted his arms around her again, strong and supportive. She wanted his mouth in her hair, on her own lips, so badly that her chest felt tight.

And she wanted her dragon back.

She'd never realized how deep a part of her the dragon was, how much of her steadiness and certainty was the familiar voice in the back of her head. She felt like all of her strength had been leached out of her, like the air had no power to fill her lungs.

After a time, Tray's one-sided conversation fell to nothing. He continued to stroke her hand through the comforter for a while longer, then stood quietly and moved away from the bed to rustle his way to the couch.

Leinani lay still, eyes closed, letting the general misery wash over her weighted limbs. The emptiness made her realize at last that more was missing than her dragon.

She couldn't feel Tray in her head any longer.

The weird echo of his emotions, usually so tightly entwined with her own, was conspicuously absent without her dragon reminding her how wonderful he was, how perfect for her. The spell *had* abated, and where she ought to feel relieved, she only felt despair, because all of his feelings and the echoes of their potential future had been replaced by her own.

Her love for him wasn't only *possible* now, it was undeniable.

He had clearly escaped the spell with only platonic affection, Leinani realized, just as they had agreed to, and she was a confused mix of happy for him and heartbroken. He had managed what she had failed, and she envied him his peace of mind. Would he remember their might-have-been with fondness? Or just be relieved that he'd escaped a terrible entanglement? Hot tears escaped beneath her eyelashes, but she refused to move to wipe them away, not wanting to disturb Tray as he settled onto the couch. She had distance pinky promised not to cry.

And failed at that, too.

She wasn't sure how long she lay there in a half-stupor of unhappiness before she finally rolled over, listening to see if Tray stirred. He was still, his breathing even.

She crawled across the bed to the window and sat up to look out.

The sky was already bright; Tray said he had no trouble sleeping in daylight, thanks to his experience with summer nights lit with midnight sun, but Leinani wasn't sure how to do the same.

She stared out at the hateful landscape that their world had shrunk to.

I am encumbered, she thought, twisting Fask's ring on her finger. *I am hopelessly encumbered, and it's not my dragon's fault, or the damned Compact. It's just me, crazy about this great guy who has been my lifeline through a terrible time.*

She let herself look at him, sleeping across the coffee table on the couch, and ached at how dear he looked, even slack in exhausted slumber, sprawled ungracefully under a blanket that barely covered him. She shivered, and realized that some of her own discomfort was that her dragonless body was cold. She had taken her dragon for granted, her easy strength, her ability to heal and shift, her immunity to minor discomfort. Everything about her life had been so easy and straight-forward. She hadn't recognized how much she had to be grateful for until she lost it all.

Leinani rubbed a hand across her cheek, still gazing at Tray as he slept, but her tears had already dried on her cheeks. He was so good, and so strong, and so kind. She loved him more deeply than she had ever even imagined loving anyone.

Now that the mate spell was gone, she could let herself feel all the things she'd fought so hard against, knowing that they would stay safely in her own mind. She could sit here on the bed, wrap the comforter around her shoulders, and adore him with all of her aching heart.

There was a far-off echo, a familiar whisper, and knowing that her dragon was returning to her was a jolt of painful hope, even if she knew it would be several hours before the rejoining was complete.

Tray stirred then, and Leinani drew a deep breath in and settled her nerves before he could wake. Whatever she felt for him, he didn't return. He had been more disciplined than she had, and she wasn't going to add guilt to his burden because she had feelings that he didn't.

He didn't wake, only turned a little and tucked the blanket under his chin.

Leinani sat and comforted herself by watching him sleep until her dragon was back, anxious and furious and familiar.

28

There was something different about Leinani, Tray thought. She had her dragon back, but she was quieter, more withdrawn. He worried for her, and tried to involve her in conversation or games, but she only smiled sadly at him and said she'd rather read.

She seemed more cheerful the following day, if not quite back to her usual relentless optimism, and Tray tried to make up for it by being twice the ham he usually was.

When they brushed against each other accidentally while making lunch a few days later, she didn't startle at all, or pull away, just looked curiously at where their elbows were touching.

She was over it, Tray thought in despair. The spell was gone and she was realizing that they didn't need to be so careful around each other anymore.

Except that he *did* have to be careful, because he didn't have even a portion of her resolve, and he wanted her now more than ever. He caught himself remembering, over and over again, how good she felt in his arms, how perfectly she fit there, how her hair smelled and how it flowed like silk over her back. Her lips were even more inviting now, as she looked quizzically at him, and he had to force himself to grin and elbow her in the side like a sibling would.

"Look what I can do now!" he joked.

She smiled slowly back at him, but he could tell that the strain of their living conditions was starting to weigh on her.

"When do you think we'll get our chance?" she asked, as they sat across from each other with their bland noodle soup cups.

They had assessed the furniture in the room and decided which pieces would make the best weapons. They reluctantly agreed that there was no escaping through the window and scaling down the hotel. They didn't have enough bedding to construct a rope and Leinani was worried that the strength of anything that they could make wouldn't be equal to their weight anyway. "I didn't know that they even made sheets with a thread count of three," she scoffed. All of their sheets and blankets together wouldn't be long enough to get them to the ground safely anyway.

It was ironic that all the powers of their dragons would make the escape simple, but it was the powers of those same dragons that kept them trapped so completely.

So they would have to fight their way past the guards and hope that they were reluctant to shoot Amara's favorite new power sources. And they still didn't know what Scoff's fancy, engraved rifle might do.

Surprise was their best weapon, and it wasn't much of one.

"It's been a few days since she took your dragon now," Tray said. "I'd honestly expected to have her dragging one of us down for our dragon-sucking spa treatment any moment now."

Leinani looked thoughtfully down at the listening ring on her finger. "There's been chatter about something big coming up. Something timed with New Years, a speech at least, and celebration. Some kind of call to action, and a prize. Maybe she'll want both of our dragons for that."

"I hate to say I hope so," Tray said wryly, "but I hope so."

"Noisy fireworks and celebration might hide some of the noise we might make," Leinani said. She spread her fingers and played with her other ring, her sparkling engagement ring, and Tray felt a wave of despair that was entirely his own. "And hopefully everyone would be busy with Amara and her show-off spells."

What was the point of escaping, when he was going to lose her at the end of it? He might have been able to stand it all if they could still be friends, but Tray didn't think he was a big enough man to watch her marry his brother. The idea of it made him feel like he was breathing ice crystals. He'd have to leave the country. There was no place in Alaska that wouldn't be too close to her. He wasn't sure which torture would be worse—having to watch her at his brother's side or leaving her forever.

He stifled a laugh. After being trapped in this little room with her for so long, he still couldn't bear the idea of being away from her. She was his fragile sanity, his sole saving grace.

But she wasn't *his*.

"What's funny?" Leinani asked, scooping out the last drops of her soup with a fragile plastic spoon. "Not this ridiculously salty soup," she said with a frown. "I will be so happy to never see a styrofoam cup again in my life. I want a cup of coffee in an actual cup again, first thing when I get home. With real cream, not powdered, dairy-free whatever-that-is."

It was a game they often played together, comparing all the outrageous and mundane things they wanted to do first when they escaped: television, books they hadn't read a dozen times already, looking up something on the Internet, putting on chapstick, swimming (Leinani), wrestling with dogs (Tray)...it was a list that would take a book to fill, with all the little things they had taken for granted for so long.

"I think I might get a degree when we get out," Tray proposed. "Rian's got some kind of highfalutin literature diploma on the wall that I've always been a little jealous of. Do they give degrees in plain old *being awesome*? I could probably get some kind of honorary degree in that."

Leinani giggled and Tray was glad to see a spark of her usual spirit. He would *miss* making her laugh. "Pretty sure you can get one of those online for twenty Kingdom Crowns," she teased him.

"What would you go to school for?" Tray asked her, suddenly curious. "I mean, if you suddenly got a bee up your butt to do it."

Leinani tilted her head, the way she had probably been coached in princess school because it was so adorable. "I think...psychology."

"Psychology?" That hadn't been in Tray's top ten guesses. He loved that she could still surprise him.

She looked at him slyly. "So I can name a traumatic disorder after us, of course. A Leinani Noodle Soup Syndrome, or a Tray Granola Wrapper Derangement."

"Oo," Tray said eagerly, "I get a *derangement*."

"I'm guessing it wasn't that far for you to fall," Leinani teased him.

Tray mimed the spoon stabbing his heart. "Oh, I'm

feeling the love now," he joked, before he realized that the words were just a little too close to the truth.

Leinani stood swiftly to clear their lunch trash, and Tray told himself that it was just coincidence, not that his humor had fallen terribly flat.

29

Leinani felt like they were both wound to nearly breaking by the time that their captors came for Tray again. Boxing Day had given them a benchmark, so she was surprised to count the days to New Year's Eve before they heard the telltale *cachink* at the keypad for the door. Deliveries usually, but not always, knocked, but they were already braced for being called.

"Oh, look," Tray said drolly. "It's Scowl and Constipation! Is Amara inviting me for tea again?"

The guards' faces didn't betray anything but the slightly smug glow of satisfaction that Amara's followers all seemed to have. "Let's go, your highness."

Leinani and Tray both stood, and the guards gestured for Tray.

Leinani fought back her instinct to protect him at any cost and watched his face as he gathered himself. For one brief moment, he glanced at her and smiled lovingly, his silvery eyes soft and unguarded, then he turned it into his trademarked grin and shrugged.

The moment shook her resolve. Was it only friendly affection? Had it been the tiniest glimpse of something more?

He was already striding away, joking with the guards about handcuffs and safewords.

The room was always achingly empty without him, somehow huge and tightly confining at the same time, and Leinani hated it passionately.

She was toying with her ring—her engagement ring—when the other ring gave its little buzz for attention. She slipped it off and held it eagerly to her ear.

It was curious to hear Tray's voice through the ring; it had never activated during his prior sessions with Amara, though Leinani wasn't sure why. Did it not consider those conversations important? Maybe because he was there to report it? Why was this one different?

"A little tighter," he was telling one of the guards mockingly. "Yeah, that's good, oh, yeah."

Ham, Leinani thought, smiling.

"Tell me, Mackenzie, when this one will fade?" Amara sounded annoyed.

"It should last a few hours longer than the last one, Leader Amara," Mackenzie said quietly. "But we're hitting a point of diminishing returns."

"Yay, more quality time with the inside of my own head," Tray quipped.

"Unless the dragon has no vessel to return to," Amara said, her voice calculating.

Leinani felt her blood run cold and Tray was uncharacteristically quiet.

"We don't know that killing the prince would leave the power indefinitely in the vessel," Mackenzie said swiftly. "It could simply dissipate."

"You can't tell?"

"It's not a potential outcome that is addressed directly by the spell. There's no way to predict it; it would be chaos magic."

"We have another dragon," Amara pointed out. "It is an experiment we could risk."

"Yes, Leader," Mackenzie agreed, her voice strangely neutral.

Leinani tasted copper and realized that she had bitten her lip. If Amara *killed* Tray…

Her dragon was as furious as she was, prepared to batter herself against the room spell to escape and save him, if that's what it took. Leinani had to fight to control both of them. Amara hadn't said which of them she would kill.

"We'll hold it as a last option," Amara said, and the ring went still beside Leinani's ear.

A last option wasn't good enough. They had to get out of here, now, as soon as possible. Leinani couldn't believe she would ever be so desperate to have her dragon wrenched away from her, but no other escape seemed possible.

Her dragon was distressed. *I do not want to go! I should not! I guard the bridge!*

You will be back, Leinani tried to comfort her. *You will always be back.*

Unless Leinani died first.

Leinani was staring at her hands without seeing them, and she gradually focused on the diamond. She could never marry Fask, not even if she and Tray somehow escaped. That future was closed to her now.

She slipped the ring off her finger and put it in the middle of the coffee table.

Freedom was a thing she had thought of frequently, over the weeks that she had been imprisoned. It meant so many things now. Freedom from the vows that had weighed so heavily on her. Freedom from the spell that had tried to mold her into its own shape. Freedom from this awful, beige hotel room. Freedom to follow her own heart.

With dry eyes, Leinani changed into the tailored clothing she'd been wearing when she arrived, and she finger-combed her hair and pinched her cheeks, remembering Tray's eyes, that last glance he'd given her. Surely she had imagined the emotion there.

When the guards brought Tray back, she wasn't waiting in the chair with tea like she usually was, out of the way of accidental touches, but leaning against the back of the couch with her arms crossed.

"Your turn, your highness," one of the guards told her, to no one's surprise. Leinani didn't notice which one, because she had eyes only for Tray, who was gazing at her intensely.

This was it, the moment they'd been waiting for. They would both be without their dragons and able to escape the room spell. Freedom would be theirs for the taking, if they were lucky enough and played their cards cleverly. She shifted her weight onto her feet and smoothed her pants down as if she was straightening a ballgown.

She and Tray passed very close to each other, and she impulsively put out her hand to him. He was watching for it and for one sweet moment, their fingers were entangled. She paused, facing him, and for a giddy second, thought he was going to kiss her. The hope was like sweet wine and dark chocolate.

Then she was being hustled out of the room and he was letting her fingers go at the end of his outstretched arm.

Was it possible, what she saw in his face, or was it her own longing that painted his features? Could he love her? Did she dare to believe it could be?

The idea buoyed her down the long, dismal hallway of the hotel.

30

Watching them take Leinani was no easier the second time than the first, even knowing it would get them closer to their goal. Tray wondered if he should put on a show, try to protest her summons, but then she unexpectedly put her hand in his and he could only think that everything he had ever wanted in the world could be his.

Before he could decide what to do with the rush of hope in his heart, she was being marched past him and away, and he couldn't chase her out into the hall without taking off his necklace and betraying their plan.

He stood with clenched fists, staring at the door as it swung closed behind her, and then turned into the room. This was their chance. He needed to be ready.

Then he drew up in surprise.

Leinani's engagement ring was glittering in the middle of the coffee table.

Hope was a shot of lightning in his chest where his dragon had lived.

He sank onto the sagging couch, staring at it in consternation.

Was this a signal of some sort? Did it mean something besides the obvious? Was she really rejecting the engagement?

Tray stood up and put his fingers at the string necklace that was meant to restrain the dragon he didn't—for the moment—have. It was tempting just to rip it off, but he would wait, and maintain the illusion of control until they brought Leinani back.

He left the ring untouched on the table and turned to do the rest of the preparation for their escape.

There was relatively little to do. He dragged the bedside table out to a place where they could easily dismantle it when the time came, and changed into the clothing he'd originally been captured in. Was it too much of a giveaway, that they were both back in these clothes? It wasn't like they weren't a big part of their usual rotation; their clothing options were still very limited.

He was folding the rest of their clothing, lacking anything more useful to do, when he heard their return, and the door latch clicked again; they had gotten efficient about the process. Tray guessed that it was a few hours before midnight. He could hear fireworks, occasionally, and once in a while, cheers and shouts.

If Leinani looked subdued upon her return, Tray knew it was an act the moment her dancing eyes met his. This was their chance, their golden opportunity, and it took every ounce of their control to wait until the door had latched again before they sprang into action.

"It's done," Leinani said, reaching to undo her necklace. When she fumbled the clasp, Tray stepped forward to do it as she held her hair away from her neck. Then he turned and let her untie his own necklace, cursing over the clumsy knots he'd put in it.

Her neck looked alluringly bare, when they were facing each other again, necklaces in hand.

"Finally," Tray said quietly.

They destroyed them, using the tiny sewing kit scissors to saw through the cords and pry open the links of Leinani's choker. Tray smashed each of his carved wooden beads, and Leinani scratched out everything she could on hers, leaving it as smashed and deformed as she could. She set the pieces down next to Fask's ring, which Tray hadn't dared to ask about.

"I won't be marrying your brother," she said quietly, looking up to catch his gaze. "There's no use in continuing to pretend that I'm going to be the queen. I couldn't be in the ceremony, there's no point in it. The Compact wouldn't recognize me as Fask's queen; it already found me a mate."

"Spells fade," Tray reminded her faintly. Was she still under its thrall? Had it lingered in her heart longer than his?

"The spell is gone," Leinani said. "But the encumbrance *isn't*. I love you, Tray. I didn't mean to, and honestly, I didn't want to. But what I feel for you is real, and not even the Compact could fix that now." She smoothed the front of her pants, as if she were wearing the fancy tapa cloth dress that she first met him in. "You don't have to return the feelings and I hope that telling you doesn't harm our...friendship. Nothing has to change."

But *everything* had changed, and there was hope shining in her golden eyes when she bravely lifted her gaze. Even if he couldn't feel it, Tray could recognize it there, and his own desire swelled in his own chest.

She loved him.

He froze too long, marveling in the realization, and she lowered her gaze with a flash of dismay. "Please don't feel bad if you don't reciprocate. I am a grown woman quite capable of maintaining a level of professional—"

Tray forgot there was a coffee table between them and nearly fell into her tripping over it. She reached automatically to catch him, and they stared at each other a moment, arms clasped. "Leinani," he murmured. "*Darling* Leinani. I thought you'd escaped, but I certainly didn't."

They crashed together desperately, her mouth tipped up to meet his as he gathered her tightly into his arms. *Ours*, he thought, and it echoed briefly in the empty place his dragon had been.

Her kiss was everything Tray had imagined it would be, her arms wound around his neck as she pressed herself hungrily against him. "Leinani," he said again, against her lips. "I love you."

The sound she made was delight and agreement and desire. Her arms slipped away, giving Tray a moment of dismay until he realized that she was trying to unbutton his shirt. That was all the invitation he needed to sweep her into his arms and carry her to the couch, barking his shins on the forgotten coffee table again.

"The bed," she suggested breathlessly as he lay her down on the couch. "It's bigger..." She managed to say that as she dragged one hand across the cock that was bulging in his pants. Tray growled and pressed down on her, kissing her neck and struggling with her shirt. He got it halfway off her before she took over, slipping it off over her head. For a moment, all he could do was stare in appreciation. "You've been driving me crazy," he admitted, not daring to touch. "Straight barking mad."

"Touch me," she begged. "Please touch me!"

Tray didn't need a second invitation, dipping his head

to kiss down her neck to the place between her breasts as he slipped one hand behind her to draw her closer. The lace of her bra tickled his face and she moaned in a way that made his hands clutch at her reflexively.

"The bed," she said again, and in the same breath, Tray said, "The bed."

Giggling, they struggled up off the couch, Leinani taking her turn to rap her shins on the coffee table and curse, then they were flying across the room for the bed, stripping off their clothing as they went.

31

When Tray said her name, soft and low and desperate, Leinani thought she might crumble, but when he said he loved her, her world felt rebuilt, in a strange new pattern where she might actually get everything she had ever desired.

She automatically reached for the dragon that wasn't there for confirmation, expecting the presence she'd lived with all her life, and when it wasn't there, had a moment of grief, which only seemed to heighten the intensity of everything else she was feeling. This was only her, all of her, raw and alone...except for Tray, who *loved* her.

He was touching her, at last, in all the ways that she'd been dying to have him touch her, fingers along the bare skin of her side, running up her back, tangling in her hair. He stroked her arms, and cupped her jaw, all while he kissed her dizzy and she clutched at him and tried to claim every inch of his skin for her own.

They fell onto the bed, crawling back so that he was covering her, heavy and safe, the bed dipping around them.

"Tray!" she cried, pressing herself up at him. They

were both still wearing jeans, somehow, and his need for her filled them, but when she scrambled to unbutton him, he stopped her, breathing hard.

"Not yet," he begged. "Not yet."

He drew her hands back up above her head and kissed her, holding her wrists down, then trailed more kisses down her neck as he traveled to linger a moment at her bare breasts, kissing and sucking until Leinani was whimpering and squirming.

He let go of her to work his way further down yet, and Leinani kept her hands up as he unbuttoned her pants and drew them over her hips as she lifted them to help him.

He kissed the curves of her hips as he pushed the jeans and underwear down to her knees, baring her, the caress of air almost as alarming as the touch of his mouth as he licked and suckled and Leinani cried out and writhed. His fingers—clever fingers!—found her folds and slowly entered her, first one, then a second, and he drew her up on a wave of pleasure that held its crest impossibly long and impossibly strong.

When her orgasm faded, she didn't feel finished, and she squirmed to take off the pants still pinning her legs, unhelpfully trying to get Tray as naked as she was. He stripped off the rest of his own clothing, and she was arrested a moment at the amazing sight of him, naked and hard, as ready for her as she was for him.

"Tray…" she murmured, reaching for his waist, for the fascinating muscles of his hips, for his arms. He was made of places she wanted to touch, and she didn't seem to have enough hands for it.

"Leinani," he groaned. "I love you."

Then he was on her again, and all of her skin was hungry for all of his, and he was saying it over and over again, "I love you, I love you," as if he had been trying not to for so long that it had gotten backed up like a blocked pipe.

She kissed his neck and twined her fingers into his hair, spreading her legs as they wrestled desperately together. He slipped into her so easily, so readily, and felt so right, buried deep inside her. She cried out in pleasure and protested wordlessly when he moved slightly away, and then they were moving together, effortlessly matched in rhythm and desire, until she was clutching at him and he was making a deep noise of agonizing release and her world seemed to stand still in a moment of perfect joy.

Afterwards, they lay together close, and Leinani was loath to let go of him, after having him so close without touching for so long. All of her skin tingled in satisfaction.

"We should be planning our escape," he said reluctantly. "It's nearly full dark."

"I know," Leinani said. It was weird to think of a world outside of these walls, after all these weeks. She tugged on the beard at his jaw. It was softer than she'd thought it would be, and although her mouth burned from so many kisses, the rest of her skin hadn't been irritated by it. It was tickly. "Let's get the hell out of here."

"Yes, your highness," Tray said flippantly. "As your highness requires."

"My highness requires a shower first," Leinani said, still unwilling to untangle herself from Tray's body. "And perhaps another kiss…"

He obliged, rolling her onto her back to rub his entire body against hers as he kissed her dizzy once more, tapering away to little feather kisses that ended on her nose.

"My highness finds that acceptable," Leinani said breathlessly.

They might not have ended there, but suddenly outside

there was a spatter of fireworks, and they frowned at each other and moved reluctantly apart. It was early yet, the sun just barely at the horizon, but they knew that their opportunity to act would be soon.

She left one kiss on his shoulder and took herself off to the bathroom where she stared at herself in the mirror as the water heated. She didn't look like a princess, naked. She looked like a wild island woman, stronger and curvier than fashion dictated, her long dark hair loose around her face. No jewels. No intricately-embroidered tapa cloth. Her nails were a disaster of chips and a range of different lengths. She hadn't been able to shave anything in more than a month, and didn't have the special skin creams and careful makeup, but she liked herself better without them anyway, if only because *this* was the woman that Tray loved.

She closed her eyes and hugged herself tightly.

Tray loved her.

It wasn't a spell, and it wasn't a compulsion, he just loved her, the way that she loved him, for all the ways that they made each other better people.

She was imprisoned in a half-rate hotel room and her dragon had been stripped out of her soul, leaving her powerless and alone in her head. She had betrayed her word, broken her engagement, and abandoned her duty. And she still could not help the happiness that seemed to be bubbling up from her feet. She danced a few steps in place, raised her hands, and turned slowly in place.

"You're so gorgeous," Tray said unexpectedly from the entrance to the bathroom. "Sorry," he added unapologetically, "but you're the one who left the door open."

Leinani continued the sweep of her arms for the dance, and finished in a practiced pose. "If I had done that sooner would we have gotten here faster?" she asked.

He remained silent and Leinani answered her own question. "No, I know we wouldn't have. It had to be us, not a spell, not a compulsion. And...I made a promise. I had to at least *try* to keep it."

"Do you have regrets?" he asked earnestly.

Leinani shook her head. "I was a different person when I made those vows," she said quietly. "And I can't regret anything that led to...this. To you. To *us.*"

He was still naked, and he rightly took her smile as an invitation to come and gather her into his arms again. It would never get old, Leinani thought, the way he felt against her, the strength in his shoulders, the way his fingers touched her face.

"I tried," he said in wonder, turning her back to the mirror, which was starting to steam over. "I tried so hard not to fall for you. You're just so sexy and funny and smart and despite being super hot, you're still actually nice." He grinned at her foggy reflection. "And you were all but *throwing* yourself at me. Not that I blame you, of course, I'm pretty irresistible."

Leinani laughed. "You are unbelievable! The real wonder here is that I fell for you! With your massive ego and your hockey-player manners and your horrible scruffy beard."

"Hey, don't dig on the beard," Tray protested, as she tugged on it. "He's got feelings!"

Leinani leaned in and kissed the shaggy fringe apologetically. "Sorry, beard. Sorry you got attached to this lunk."

"I take back everything I said about you being nice," Tray said, and then he was lifting her up onto the bathroom counter and kissing her again.

"The water is running," Leinani said, kissing him back just as eagerly. "I hate to waste it."

"Easy fix," Tray said, and he almost dropped her trying to carry her to the shower; it was a sobering reminder that neither of them had their dragon-augmented strength.

They soaped each other slowly and thoughtfully, exploring each other in agonizing detail. All those places that she'd tried not to look, the lines of muscle and the angles of his jaw. They were, for the moment at least, hers, just as she was his.

By the time they were clean, he was hard again, and she was wet and eager. They made slow love, touching and kissing and laughing and tickling, through every position that Leinani knew. He brought her to new levels of pleasure, where time stood still and her whole world was narrowed to how he filled her and his mouth and his noises and the way that all of her skin was on fire for his touch.

Their second shower was much swifter. Outside, the firecrackers were still going periodically as the hour grew gradually closer to midnight. They each dressed carefully, checking and double-checking their laces and buttons. Tray added a few extra stitches to the button he'd replaced.

"Will it matter?" Leinani asked dubiously.

"If we fail to escape because my stitching was substandard, I will never forgive myself," Tray said soberly.

If they failed to escape.

If they failed to escape, she had everything to lose now, Leinani realized. They had to get out, both of them, in one piece. She couldn't bear to think of any other option.

32

They scoured the little room for anything they needed to bring, and set up their decoy. Tray tucked his soap-wrapper flower carefully into a back pocket and Leinani shoved Brett the Button-eyed into the top of her jeans, cursing useless women's pockets.

"You don't have to take it," Tray told her. "I could make you a new one when we get home."

"We all escape together," she told him. "I'm not leaving Brett behind."

"Is that a sockpuppet in your pants," Tray asked slyly, "or are you just happy to see me?"

Leinani laughed, and rewarded him with a slow, lingering kiss. "You tell me…"

He ransacked the Dating Game box and found his scruffy avatar, putting it in the opposite pocket from the flower.

Leinani turned the sewing kit over in her hands. "It could be useful?" she said, taking the scissors out.

"You have pocket space?" Tray asked. Leinani reluctantly put it aside.

There was something intensely satisfying about dismantling the bedside table to make them both weapons, the worst of their noise covered by the increasing percussion of the fireworks outside; most of the show was on the other side of the hotel and they could only see the light reflecting off the snow-frosted mountains.

They weren't particularly sophisticated weapons, but Tray thought he could probably lay someone out with a good blow, even without his dragon strength, and he'd long since learned not to underestimate Leinani. She had a determined look in her profile as she tested her swing and found the best way to hold the block of wood.

Leinani made one final sweep of the room, opening drawers, drawing her fingers over the back of the chairs, and they were ready to go.

"Now?" she said, returning from her circuit.

"Now," Tray said.

He remembered at the last moment that he could actually touch her, and when he reached for her, she startled a moment as if she had forgotten, too. Then they were embracing tight, clinging to each other desperately, and it was almost as much pleasure as the sex, just to have her in his arms.

She was his, and he was hers, and they would get out of here together, Tray told himself.

They could only gauge the time by the increasing fireworks, and had to guess that the new year was approaching fast. He finally let her go, and stepped back, into the blind spot that Leinani had arranged in the room so long ago.

Leinani drew a shuddering breath and let it out in an impressive scream, standing beside the bed where they had swaddled a couch cushion and extra pillows in blankets. It wouldn't fool anyone up close, but it didn't have to.

For a moment, nothing happened outside the closed

door and Tray's heart sunk. Their plan relied on drawing the guards inside. They wouldn't have as much of an element of surprise trying to get out into the hallway to attack. Leinani continued to scream, weeping and crying, "Help! Oh, help!"

Like the dummy, it wasn't an acting job that would have stood up to great scrutiny, but they were both relieved to hear the snick-snick of the door lock.

"He won't wake up!" Leinani cried in affected anguish. Then, in case it wasn't obvious enough, she appealed to their sense of fear. "Amara will be so angry if he dies!"

That brought them in, and as soon as the first of them stepped into Tray's view, he attacked.

He had been in plenty of brawls with his brothers, and he'd fought in hockey matches, always holding back his true strength.

This fight was completely different.

He had none of his dragon strength, and he had no interest in holding *anything* back. He brought his wooden club down on the first guard's head so hard it splintered, and the guard staggered and dropped his gun, but didn't fall. The second guard, Scoff, was holding the engraved rifle, and Tray ignored the first to tackle Scoff in earnest, suspecting that it would do them the most damage if he had a chance to use it.

Leinani rocketed over the back of the couch into the fray, snatching her own club up from the coffee table where it had been waiting. She hit furiously at the first guard that Tray had struck, not doing a great deal of damage, but effectively keeping him from joining in Tray's struggle.

And it was a struggle. Scoff was strong, and he had a weapon, even if he couldn't bring it to bear. He got several good hits in with the butt of the rifle, enough to make

Tray's eyes sting before he got up under it and gave the guard a staggering uppercut.

Scoff's grip on the rifle slackened and Tray was able to wrestle it away and use it back against him as a club. Leinani made a noise of pain then; her own opponent was regaining his balance and had scored a hit on her.

Tray was too occupied to figure out where she'd been hurt, but knowing that she had been gave him extra strength and speed. He gave Scoff a tremendous hit with the rifle that made something crunch, and turned to clip the other guard in the head, sending him falling to the side. He had enough time to see Leinani pounce down on him, and then Scoff was attacking again, and Tray's attention was only on keeping himself from being pummeled.

He was able, at last, to turn his blocks into hits and knock Scoff back into the desk, which broke. Tray followed him down, and it was several moments before he realized he was straddling the guard and hitting his unconscious body.

"Tray?"

Leinani was kneeling on the other guard, pulling her club back from his neck where he'd been pressing it. "Did I...?" she asked in horror, just as he took a gargling breath. His eyes remained closed.

It was still and tense, both of them panting in shock.

"Are you...okay?" Tray asked. He wished he could tell.

"I'm okay," Leinani promised grimly, wrenching her gaze away from the prone guard as she stood. "I'm okay enough. Let's go."

This was their chance. Probably their only chance.

Tray clenched his hands around Scoff's gun and stood up, reaching for Leinani's hand.

Clutching each other, they went for the doorway, the entrance to their prison for so long. The door had half closed behind the guards, and Tray pushed it open the rest of the way with the butt of his gun.

They walked through together, so close that Tray could feel Leinani trembling at his side. The hallway was empty, but they could hear voices somewhere out of sight.

"We're free," Leinani whispered. "We're free."

"Not yet," Tray cautioned. "Let's go." They went right, a direction they'd never gone, where an exit sign promised a stairwell at the end of the hall.

Torn between wrenching the door open for speed and opening it slowly for caution, Tray was alarmed when the stairwell door opened under its own power, and they were suddenly face-to-face with Mackenzie, who looked as surprised as they were.

He stepped back just far enough to raise the gun. "Back away," he said, but Mackenzie only frowned at him. She turned and looked back down the stair, and Tray could only think that she was going to call for help, hesitating only a moment before pulling the trigger.

Leinani gave a cry of dismay and looked away, but Tray heard the click of the gun and watched a wave of light wash over Mackenzie, doing absolutely nothing at all.

She stepped back in shock and shook her head. "I was just coming to get you," she said, raising both of her empty hands. "I see that you realized that your necklaces wouldn't work without your dragons. I told Amara that they would, so she thinks you are still imprisoned."

Leinani and Tray stared at her, and the door started to close on her. They both startled as Mackenzie caught it, and gestured them down the stairwell. "Let's go."

Tray slowly lowered the rifle. "What are you doing?"

"I'm getting you out of here," Mackenzie said.

"Why?" Leinani wanted to know.

Mackenzie paused, but Tray didn't think it was the

kind of pause where she was thinking of a lie to convince them, but a struggle of emotion. "I can't let her do this anymore," she finally said. "And I feel like I have to. You have powerful friends, maybe if you're free you can *stop* her from hurting anyone else. The guards won't stay out long, and Amara is ready for her big show at the amphitheater, we'll go down the back stairs and get out while they are distracted, this is our chance, come on."

As they went down the echoing stairs, Mackenzie told them, "Amara is planning a big offensive soon. She's whipping everyone into a frenzy of hatred, and the dark web is full of plots and plans. She's got contacts in the royal courts, although apparently your newest sister did manage to get a bunch of her accounts frozen and let me tell you, she wasn't happy about that. I don't have a lot of information, because Amara is pretty tight-lipped, but I have the call names of some of her contacts. You'll want to keep an eye on the Internet using the keyword Dusk Cause."

"Can you tell us all of this later?" Tray wanted to know, as they came to the next floor. There was the sound of a clanking door somewhere, and voices below. "Like when we're well away?" he muttered.

"I'm only taking you to the exit of the compound," Mackenzie whispered back. "I...can't leave."

"Don't you want to?" Leinani wanted to know. A door closed several stories below them and the voices grew more quiet. Tray slowly shut the door behind them and they crept down the echoing stairs as quietly as they could manage.

"More than anything," Mackenzie confessed.

"Won't she be pissed that you let us go?" Tray asked.

"If you'll hush, she won't know," Mackenzie hissed. "Shhh!" They were at the landing between floors now.

On the floor below them, a door loudly opened and they could hear angry shouting.

"Back up!" Mackenzie hissed, turning to push them back up the steps. "Up, shhh!"

But the door they'd just passed flew open and banged against the wall. "Down here!" someone called.

33

Leinani knew she should be terrified. They were dragonless, trapped in an indefensible stairwell, and armed only with a few pieces of broken furniture and a magic gun that didn't work. Tray would be good to have in a fistfight but she was doubtful that Mackenzie would be much help, even if her loyalty had actually shifted. And the guards had real guns.

But her free hand was in Tray's, and he *loved* her, and Leinani could not forget that, even when she ought to be in fear for her very life.

He squeezed her tighter, and then took his hand back so he could use both on his useless rifle like a club.

"Surrender," Scowl said, as he led the guards down from above. Constipation was leading the guards from below, and Leinani did not have to be a great tactician to know that they didn't stand a chance. The stairwell was hollow down the middle, but it was still at least four stories down, and she could hear that there were other forces at the bottom now, too.

She lowered her club, even as Tray raised his and

braced himself for battle. "Nothing foolish needs to happen here," she said, in her best press voice. "We are clearly outnumbered and outgunned." She put a hand on Tray's arm and he reluctantly put the gun down. Neither of them offered to drop their weapons, and the guards did not lower their guns.

There was a moment of impasse while Leinani wracked her brain for any leverage she might have.

But it was Mackenzie who spoke. "Frank," she said gently, stepping in front of Tray and Leinani with her hands spread peacefully.

Scowl flinched. "That's not my name."

"It was," Mackenzie said sorrowfully. "You lived in Detroit. You had a wife."

Frank-Scowl's hand tightened on his gun and he seemed to steel himself. "I have The Cause now. The Cause is my family."

Leinani stayed quiet, but was glad when Tray found her hand again, switching his gun to a single-handed grip and keeping it at his side.

"Amara is wrong to do this," Mackenzie said. "She can't—"

But at Amara's name, Frank's face went into his familiar scowl. "You aren't the favored one now," he snarled at her, and then he closed the space between them and smashed Mackenzie in the face with the butt of his gun.

She staggered back and Leinani dropped her club catching her slight form.

It was over swiftly after that, and Leinani begged Tray not to fight as they were swarmed by the guards and she was pinned.

He only hit one of them before they were all frog-marched—to Leinani's surprise—*down* the stairwell, not back up to their room.

"Where are you taking us?" Leinani wanted to know, trying not to stumble as they were rushed ahead. She heard gunshots as they arrived at the bottom step, then realized that they were fireworks; the show was starting in earnest now.

They were jerked through a heavy metal door and were suddenly outside. Outside was so unexpected that Leinani forgot to walk and was dragged several steps before she could make her legs move again.

There was sky above, glorious sky, and fresh air, and Leinani drew in deep, surprised breaths at the way it felt in her lungs. She was cold, without her dragon to warm her, and she had forgotten how a breeze felt as it lifted her hair and raised goosebumps on her arms.

The hotel, from the outside, was designed in a very obviously Greek or Minoan style, with ostentatious columns and molding in modern materials.

They were hauled briskly along the side of the building and around to an amphitheater filled with people. Angry people. They were shouting and chanting, and there were fireworks overhead.

A stage waited, and the guards drew to a stop and waited at the side as a familiar figure entered from the far side, raising her hands in the air.

Amara.

Already, there were spells activated all over the stage. Sloppy, Leinani thought. Gaudy. Even without her dragon's sensitivity, she could tell that there was a variety of enchantments, keeping the crowd in sway.

Just as she recognized it, she felt it creep up over her own senses. Amara went from a hateful figure of fear to a powerful object of worship that she could not help herself from loving.

I love Tray, she thought fiercely, trying to fight off the compulsion.

But it was no use, she was helplessly enthralled as Amara reached the podium and began to speak.

Every word she said was golden truth, beautiful destiny, precious wisdom. Leinani could not later say what she actually said, only that it was moving and inspiring. She was a better person, simply for being in this woman's presence.

"You're up, princess," Previously-Frank said, yanking her forward.

34

Tray had been in front of plenty of crowds.
He didn't love them the way Fask did, but there was something deeply satisfying about the roar of approval, the feeling of power when they cheered.

This crowd, however, had no love for him, or for Leinani, who was trying to walk with dignity between two guards who were more intent on showing their power over her, yanking her roughly across the stage. He struggled futilely with his own guards and someone threw an empty water bottle at him, striking his leg. They were taken to the front of the stage, where the crowd snarled at them in hatred.

"We unmask the demons!" Amara cried, and her audience gave a growl, raising fists and cursing. "We expose the evil among us!"

For a moment, Tray was puzzled; Amara seemed to be speaking in English and he felt compelled by her voice. Surely what she was saying could only be true, which was confusing. His dragon wasn't a demon. Then he glimpsed the papers on the podium before her.

A spell. She was casting several spells, and they weren't fading as she used them, they were actually building in strength rather than waning, and the paper wasn't burning at all. It was being fed from the dagger that lay beside it. The dagger with his demon...no, dragon. Tray shook his head in confusion.

"We heal our world and bring power to our worthy cause!" Amara said in triumph and Tray wrestled more with his complete inability to disbelieve what she was saying than he did with the guards.

She looked so wise and strong and Tray could feel the spell creeping under his skin as he failed in his efforts to deny it. She was perfection, her two whole hands in the air as she spoke, healed by the magic she had drained from him. Of course she should have that power, she was the only one who could possibly know what to do with it. She understood everything, and he was merely...mistaken. Why would he even want to refute her?

"We rid the world of the ones who would subjugate us! Do they deserve to rule? They live their lives of privilege at our expense, keeping magic from those who would use it to make your world better!"

She was right, of course. She could never be anything but right.

Then Amara pointed at Leinani. "They are evil, and must be destroyed so that we can realize our destiny."

But...Leinani wasn't evil. Tray felt like two parts of his own head had just collided.

Leinani was generous and brave and loyal.

Tray wasn't sure when he'd stopped fighting his guards; they appeared as enthralled as everyone on the stage and all the people watching them. Leinani was swaying in place. Could she possibly believe the terrible things that Amara said?

Leinani should never believe such things. Somehow that was the worst of all, and Tray felt the shell of Amara's spell crack under the pressure of his protest.

"Come," Amara said, her voice full of sweet promise and unyielding command.

The princess put one slow foot in front of the other as the guards released her, walking in a daze to the cult leader.

Rage burned back the chilly magic of her spell from Tray's mind. "She is my mate," he cried, but his words felt like they echoed back at him from inside a tin can. His guards chuckled, and everyone else ignored him. Line of sight, he remembered, but he couldn't seem to close his eyes.

"Come, and meet your destiny," Amara said, sounding kind and reasonable as she raised the dagger and let it flash in the sun for the crowd's cheers.

Tray had spent more than a month fighting destiny, denying a spell that offered him everything he'd never known he wanted out of sheer stubborn will. Amara's spell was, by comparison, a surface effect, brittle like autumn ice. "She is my mate!" he cried again, pushing back against it as Leinani paused and turned slowly towards him like she was sleepwalking. "And that is my dragon!"

Tray didn't try to slip the guards holding him, he only wrenched his eyes closed at last, remembering Amara's words. His dragon was a part of him as long as he lived. And he lived for Leinani.

Come back! he called, into the void of his chest. All of his hard-won discipline was narrowed into a single purpose: to save their mate.

Amara's spell shattered and the paper on the podium burst into purple flame. Tray could feel his dragon, as if he was coalescing from ashes spread out over the crowd, drawing from the dagger, from Amara herself. He'd been spread into a million tiny shards of magic, but Tray's love for Leinani could draw him back together.

Leinani shook her head and stumbled as her eyes came awake again.

"My mate," she said in wonder, then firmer, "My dragon!"

"Shoot them χάμω!" Amara cried, knowing she was in the process of losing control. Her speech seemed to twist away from Tray's understanding, but it was clear that she was calling her men to attack.

But it was too late for them. Tray shifted, just as Leinani raised her hands to gather her own dragon back into herself.

Amara dived for Leinani, dagger lifted. Its power was draining away as their dragons reclaimed what was theirs, but it was still a sharp weapon, and Leinani was still only human.

With a roar of fury, Tray unleashed a wave of fire over the guards between them who had failed to sensibly flee at the first sight of his scaled form, careful not to flame too close to Leinani. He spread wings like huge sails and the crowd, loose from Amara's spell, began to stir and scatter in alarm. Screams filled the little amphitheater. There was a spray of bullets; some of Amara's guards had higher ground, behind and above the audience. Tray was dismayed to see Leinani fall to the ground...and then rise snarling and flaming in her dragon form as Amara fled.

Dragons were not armored against bullets, though a single shot was unlikely to kill one; they had dense hide and thick muscle. Tray felt them sting into his side, and enough of them would shred his wings to uselessness. He roared to Leinani and sprang into the air, praying that she would follow him.

To his dismay, she paused, bowled into the remaining guards on the stage, then turned and kicked up off of the stage, something in her forepaws as she spread her wings and fled to the sky. Tray made a protective pass behind her, angling in fast and flaming an arc across the stage, his wings banking so sharply that he had to fold them in and let momentum take him up, or risk hitting the steep steps. He saw Amara, running in front of flames for the side entrance, and for a moment was tempted to hunt after her and bring her fiery justice for her crimes.

But Leinani, more sensibly, was concentrating on getting away, and Tray was not prepared to lose her, not for revenge, not ever. He gave a final burst of flame at the last guards in the highest seats and rose up in her wake, happy to have the hateful place behind him at last.

Her burden, Tray realized quickly, was Mackenzie, clinging to Leinani's gentle claws in terror and confusion as they flew. Amara would not have allowed her to live long after her betrayal, and Tray felt a moment of chagrin for realizing that he would not have paused even a second to save her.

At first, they were only flying anywhere away. Then, as they escaped from bullet range, the amphitheater shrinking beneath them, they circled, reveling in dragon form and freedom, and started to genuinely look around.

There were still some fireworks going off in most of the small communities beneath them, and Tray knew that they would look like nothing more than a brief fall of sparkles in the sky as they winged overhead. As it diminished beneath and behind them, the lit edges of the island proved their suspicion that they'd been held in Crete.

Leinani gave a bobble of her wings to get his attention and then banked, turning west, out over the dark ocean. Tray tried to compose a map in his head, and realized that she was leading them in the direction of Majorca. Majorca may not have been the greatest ally that Alaska or Mo'orea had, but they were part of the Small Kingdoms, and it would be a safe place to rest and make contact with the rest of the world again. He tried to guess distances and failed.

To his surprise, long before Italy's distinctively lit boot fell away beneath them, he became aware of dark forms flanking them in the sky. Dragons. Could they be Amara's Small Kingdom allies? He'd spent so long with enemies that he saw them everywhere.

He fleetingly considered trying to buck their escort, but he could see that Leinani, weighed down by Mackenzie, was already starting to tire, her wings slowing and her motions looking labored. How badly had she been hurt before she had been able to shift? Tray could feel his own strain; their weeks of captivity and his constant separation from his dragon had weakened them both. Now that the adrenaline of fighting and escaping was beginning to fade, he was aware that his side felt hot where several shots had hit true.

Their dragon guards seemed to consider this, and one took point in a few swift wingbeats and turned to lead them down to an island just off of Italy.

Not Small Kingdoms, Tray thought, his mind feeling fuzzy, but something closer. Closer sounded good.

In the darkness, Tray could see the lights of an airport landing strip, and he wondered what their sensors would make of the confusing natural cloaking that dragons wore. He was too weary to question the sensibility of landing, and followed their leader without balking, crashing into the ground harder than he intended and turning to find Leinani landing rather more gracefully, back winging as she landed deliberately on her back legs and slowly released the limp form of Mackenzie...to collapse on her side, shifting back to human as she went.

Tray leaped for her in dragon form, landing beside her in human shape and drawing her into his arms as their escorts shifted more sedately.

35

Leinani hoped that she'd been able to put Mackenzie down gently enough not to harm her, but the last moments of their flight had been a haze of misery and pain, behind a veil of disbelief. Could she possibly be free, after so long? Could this be...real? Or was it just another cruel dream that she would wake from?

Her dragon was there in her head, whole again and reassuring, and Tray was gathering her up in a desperate, worried embrace.

Leinani burst into tears, so tired and relieved and overwhelmed that she could do nothing else, distance pinky promise or not.

"Are you hurt?" Tray demanded. "Did she hurt you?"

Leinani looked up at him, for a moment only seeing Amara, the dagger that had held their dragons in her hand, the wild look in her eyes, the fury and hatred. She blinked. "Not badly," she said, remembering the glancing blow to her shoulder. "But I was shot…"

She hadn't quite been fast enough to shift before the bullets hit, but it hadn't felt *bad*. It hadn't been anything that kept her from flying, and that was all she'd needed to do. Tray gently probed her side and she gave a hiss of pain.

"We have a medic coming," one of the strange dragon shifters said, crouching beside Tray. It was too dark to make out the insignia on his uniform. The other was kneeling by Mackenzie, who was sitting carefully and protesting weakly that she wasn't hurt badly.

"I'm just a little sick to my stomach," she insisted. "I'll be fine."

"She's been shot," one of the shifters observed.

A siren at the far end of the airport began to scream.

In the headlights of the little ambulance that came out of the darkness, there seemed to be a great deal of blood, and not all of it was Leinani's. "You were shot," she protested, trying to sit up and figure out where Tray had been hit.

"Surface wounds," Tray insisted, as a medical crew came flying out with first aid kits. None of them asked how three ragged gunshot victims came to be sitting at the end of a deserted airport runway.

"I presume it was a small personal aircraft crash?" one of the medics asked wryly. "Disoriented by fireworks, maybe?"

"We'll provide some wreckage if you need," one of the strange dragon shifters chuckled. "This is Princess Leinani of Mo'orea, and Prince Tray of Alaska, recently escaped from a crazy cult in Crete. Let's see if we can return them in one piece."

One of the medics had been cutting away the fabric at Leinani's shoulder and froze for a moment. "Your highness," she said respectfully.

Leinani was too busy gritting her teeth to answer.

"What did this?" the medic wanted to know.

"Small serrated metal dagger," Tray said briefly. "Wait, how do you know who we are, or where we were?"

"We got a tip," one of the strangers explained. "I'm Forsch, you know my half-brother Drayger."

"Talgor," the other volunteered.

"A tip?" Tray furrowed his brow.

"I went into town and sent an email to your families just after Christmas," Mackenzie explained. "I didn't think it had gotten through, I feared it had died in a spam trap." She had not offered to stand up yet.

"I hope I didn't hurt you," Leinani said. "There wasn't a lot of time to figure out a good way to carry you."

"As a method of transport, it left a lot to be desired," Mackenzie quipped. "But I don't think anything is broken." She rubbed her forearm self-consciously, and Leinani had a glimpse of a tattoo there.

Abruptly, the ring on Leinani's finger buzzed. She hesitated only a moment before she slipped the ring off and put it to her ear.

"What—"

"Shhhhh," Tray hushed them. "She's getting a call." He pointed the medic that had been fussing with his side to check work on Mackenzie while he crawled closer to Leinani.

Amara's smooth voice sent shivers up her spine and Tray leaned in close to listen with her. It was a delicious relief that he could wrap an arm around her and put his head right against hers, without worrying that they might accidentally touch. She was still hyper-aware of his closeness, but it came with all the comfort in the world now.

"Leave the monitors," Amara was saying. "Just take the laptops and the computers and whatever fits into the boxes. Our sponsor will replace anything we need at the second site. No, we don't need the chairs. Get those files! You fool, why did you trust that woman?" There were frantic sounds of scraping furniture and boxes. The sound of rustling was punctuated with the distinct squeal of a packing tape dispenser.

"You said to! You didn't want her to suspect!" Leinani wouldn't miss the sound of Scoff's voice, sounding more like Whine at the moment. "I thought that...our *royal sponsor* had lost the access to the accounts."

"Only some of it," Amara snarled. "This is his fault; he can pay it out of his hoard. Just put those in the box and mark it miscellaneous! We don't have time to sort through!"

There was a cacophony of clinks and rattles and the sounds of rustling overwhelmed the voices. There was the nearby scream of the tape roll and there was one muffled, "Idiots!" before the ring went silent.

"I think it's been packed," Tray said, as Leinani returned the ring to her finger bemusedly.

Leinani wanted to ask who the *royal sponsor* was, but she glanced at their audience cautiously and Tray didn't bring it up either. It did seem awfully convenient that Drayger's equally illegitimate brothers had found them so quickly after their escape. And how much could they trust Mackenzie, really?

"Have a good phone call?" Forsch asked slyly. "Cute trick."

"Do you have...a real phone?" Tray wanted to know. "I want to call home as soon as possible."

But when Talgor handed a cellphone over, Tray hesitated and offered it to Leinani. "Do you want to make the first call?"

Leinani took it, and stared at the screen so long that it went to sleep. So much time had gone by since she'd done normal things, like dial a phone, or talk to her mother.

What would she say? What would they think? Talgor reactivated it with his fingerprint and this time she slowly dialed the familiar number.

Her mother's assistant answered; even private numbers got screened. "Molly," Leinani said hesitantly. "It's Lei…"

Molly screamed, and there was a commotion at the other end of the line as she dropped the phone and hollered for the Queen of Mo'orea at the top of her considerable lungs.

"Leinani? Leinani?? Baby, are you okay?"

Her mother's tears unleashed her own as Leinani struggled to assure her mother, "I'm okay, Mom. I'm okay. It's…a long story, but I'm okay. We're free. I just wanted to let you know right away."

Tray's arm around her was tighter than ever, and Leinani didn't even mind the sting of her wounds.

Her mother babbled tearfully for several moments, very little of it intelligible, and Leinani continued to assure her that she wasn't hurt, exchanging a bemused look with the medic, who shrugged helplessly. "I'll be home soon," she promised, then she realized in surprise that she meant Alaska. "I'll see you in Fairbanks, Mother. Really soon. I have to go, I just had to tell you. Give my love to Daddy and the boys. Soon, I promise."

She hung up over her mother's continued protests, then handed the phone to Tray, who stared at it with the same disconnected confusion as she had. After a moment, he dialed his own numbers, and then it was her turn to comfort him as Rian answered and began shouting in relief and anxious worry. Tray was no more together than she had been and after he hung up, they simply clung to each other until Forsch cleared his throat in embarrassment.

"How about you, Miss…?" Talgor waved the phone at Mackenzie and she stared at it.

"Mackenzie. Just Mackenzie. And there's no one to call," she said quietly. "I don't know anyone outside of The Cause." She looked at Leinani and Tray then, sweeping her gaze across all of them in piercing turn. "You know people, though. You know people who can help. Will you?"

"They're free now," Forsch pointed out.

"Tray and Leinani weren't the only people that Amara was holding against their will," Mackenzie said.

"This is a Small Kingdoms matter now," Tray said, frowning. "We will see that Amara is brought to justice and that any prisoners that she still has will be freed."

"She gambled too much this time," Leinani hissed in anger. The medic was working on her side now, probing for any embedded bullets and wiping away blood. Her shirt had been cut up the side and was hanging loose on her now. "There will be a reckoning."

Mackenzie looked only slightly mollified. "She won't stay there waiting for you to come back and politely arrest her with a team of dragons," she pointed out. "They're probably pulling up stakes now, to move to a new location."

"So," said one of the medics to Talgor. "That's what, four personal aircraft wrecks we've had here in the last six months." He made air quotes around *personal aircraft wrecks*. "You guys going to want a private jet this time, too?"

Tray looked at the phone. "What time is it now?" He laughed humorlessly. "If we left now, we could make it home for the New Year's countdown in that time zone."

Leinani had to giggle at the idea. It seemed far off and impossible to think of being where they'd started this journey, thousands of miles away and a hundred lifetimes.

"You don't want to leave right now, do you?" Talgor protested. "We could put you up in a hotel for the night."

"No!" Leinani and Tray said together.

"No hotels," Tray repeated vehemently. "Mackenzie, come with us. You know Amara's plans better than anyone, and you could give us a lot of insight about her operations. You could be the key to bringing her to justice and freeing the others."

Leinani thought she was going to protest for a moment, then Mackenzie nodded. "I'd like to help however I can," she agreed.

"Let's get you guys some new clothing while they gas up the jet and get the clearance to leave," Forsch suggested. "I'll call a limo, we've got a place nearby."

Tray helped Leinani to her feet. The bandages that had been applied to her side and shoulder pulled strangely at her skin, but despite the pain, she felt light-footed and whole-hearted, at last.

They were free. They'd escaped. They were together.

"Field day for a therapist," Tray murmured near her ear merrily.

"They'll write papers about us."

"Secret papers," Tray agreed. "Dragon psychology will be a whole new underground branch. Maybe they'll name something after us. Leinani Soap Syndrome, or Malady of Tray."

"What are the symptoms?" Leinani wanted to know, leaning her head against him and wrapping an arm around as they walked to the back of the ambulance for a ride back to the terminal. They had their good sides together, and that felt just right.

"Delirious joy," Tray suggested.

"And the treatment?" Leinani let Tray help her up into the vehicle.

"Kisses," Tray said, and she leaned down to get one just as he climbed in beside her.

"No hanky-panky on the stretcher," the medic warned.

Mackenzie, limping, was helped in beside them, and she gave them a wry shake of her head.

Forsch slipped in beside them to sit on the narrow bench as the medic closed the door and walked around to the front. They left their flashing lights on, but kept the siren off as they zipped into the night.

Leinani found Tray's hand. They were *free*.

36

They all slept for most of the flight back to Alaska, in the fully reclined airline seats of the jet that the Majorcan brothers provided. They were served a meal of pasta with chicken that Leinani quoted poetry over and Mackenzie ate in quiet awe.

When they landed at last, the stillness of the plane powering down after hours of flying only added to the deep sense of disconnect.

They were greeted by an unexpectedly large honor guard, and a bite of cold air that had Mackenzie cowering into her borrowed coat as they stepped out onto the passenger stairs.

Their timing was impressive; the final round of fireworks were just starting as the clock crept towards midnight. Changing time zones only made things more surreal, Tray thought, and even the stars seemed unfamiliar, after a month of staring at the sky from their prison windows.

Fask was standing with Captain Luke and Rian at the

head of the guard and Tray felt Leinani squeeze his hand once before she started down the narrow steps before him.

He caught up with her at the base of the stairs and took her hand again before any words were spoken, exchanging a look with Fask as he did.

"There was an attempt on the life of the Queen of Siberian Islands." Luke looked like she could grind glass in her mouth. "Fairbanks is unlikely to have that kind of civil unrest, but let's not dawdle."

Fask's expression, in the poor light, was not entirely clear, but he was definitely conflicted, and not entirely happy. Tray thought he ought to feel guilty, because he'd failed in his effort to resist the mistaken mate bond, but it was impossible to feel anything could be wrong about loving Leinani.

Leinani gave a respectful dip of her head to Fask and he just as carefully returned the gesture to her.

Should he apologize? Tray wondered, but Leinani spoke first. "Our thanks for your hospitality," she opened diplomatically.

"Please make yourself welcome," Fask replied, every bit as vaguely. "All of you."

There was a round of handshaking then, as Leinani formally introduced Forsh, Talgor, and Mackenzie. Tray was barely in earshot of Captain Luke, who muttered darkly about more bastards to keep an eye on. Mackenzie looked entirely out of her depth, but kept her chin high and met Fask's gaze bravely.

"Mackenzie was instrumental in our escape," Leinani said warmly. "I believe that the information she has will be very useful in bringing Amara to justice."

Fask bowed over her hand respectfully. "Alaska's gratitude is yours," he said graciously.

"Oh, I. Of course," Mackenzie stuttered nervously. "Thank you?"

There was a moment of hesitation when it came to Tray's turn, and he thought for a bad moment that Fask was going to refuse the hand he offered.

"Brother," Fask said coldly, and Tray wondered again if he was supposed to apologize.

Then Fask clasped his hand and brought him in for a swift hug, pounding him on the shoulders. "I cannot *believe* you stole my bride."

The ice broken, Tray laughed in relief and teased, "She traded up! Who could blame her?"

Then Rian was wrapping arms around him and he was absorbing a warm bear hug from his twin brother. "Glad to have you back," Rian said sincerely. "I *knew* you didn't just elope."

"I have too much moral fiber for that," Tray laughed. He stepped back and found Leinani at his side, just where he expected her to be, and it was the most natural thing in the world to take her hand into his again. "Besides, *marriage*, ew."

It occurred to him suddenly that he and Leinani had never spoken about what would happen next. There had been no certain path while they were being held together, and there were many times he wasn't sure there was going to be a future at all. "Unless you want to get married?" he said to Leinani spontaneously.

"Are you asking me to marry you?" she asked, staring back at him with her golden eyes aglow. Overhead, the fireworks were starting to crack in earnest.

"Yeah," Tray said, the corners of his mouth curving up. "Yeah, if you want. If you will. Will you? Will you, please?"

Leinani closed her mouth and stared at him, then, for a

heart-stopping moment, turned away to Fask. "Will you release me from my vows?"

Fask hesitated just long enough for Tray's heart to skip another beat and his dragon to swirl in concern, then smiled and shook his head. "I have no claim on you," he said, sounding the tiniest bit sour.

Leinani turned back to Tray, a slow smile blooming over her face. "I will marry you," she said, as if she was granting a great favor.

Tray was sure that she was, by the leap of joy that filled him, and though he had promised himself to behave in front of Fask, he could not resist pulling Leinani into his arms to kiss her passionately.

By the time he had finished his kiss, the Majorcan brothers were laughing and wolf-whistling and everyone was piling into the waiting limo.

"Marriage, *ew*?" she teased him, while the others were out of earshot.

"It might be okay," Tray conceded. "With you. I mean, you made kidnapping and torture bearable, probably marriage would be a little better than that."

"Maybe a little more bearable than imprisonment and torment. Oh, I'm so glad we have these benchmarks." Leinani's face was alight with the same happiness that Tray felt. Even if they had no magical emotional bond, he could read her now, and he knew he would cheerfully spend the rest of his life learning all her other moods.

They kissed again, until Fask had the driver lean on the horn, then scrambled to the limo to drive home at last.

37

Leinani nearly ate herself sick at breakfast, heaping her plate with pancakes and berries and fresh, crisp bacon, and she drank two tall glasses of cold, sweet orange juice.

"It's like you haven't eaten in weeks," her mother said, and promptly burst into tears. There had been a lot of that since she and Leinani's father arrived that morning.

"Yes, Mother," Leinani said reassuringly. "I promise, I'm fine, I'm really just fine." Her bullet wounds were already mostly healed, and her shoulder only gave her moments of trouble. She had slept peacefully in Tray's arms on a bed where the mattress didn't sag and the sheets weren't even slightly itchy. She'd taken a blissfully long, hot shower in the morning, used a real hairbrush, shaved, and dressed in clothing that actually fit her.

Weirdest of all was not wearing a necklace. She wasn't sure she would willingly wear one again. Certainly not a choker.

"You aren't just fine," her mother protested, but Leinani's father took over the job of comforting her and slipped Leinani a banana behind her back. She knew that the bunch of apple bananas they'd come with had been her father's idea.

"I have a surprise for you," Tray whispered in her other ear.

While her mother was still distracted, Leinani took her banana and slipped out of her chair after Tray.

She wasn't sorry to close the door to the informal dining hall behind her, and be away from all the stares and stiff smiles. She thought she could grow to like them all quite a lot, his brothers and their mates, and she loved her parents dearly, but everyone was flustered and confused by her, and she could understand why. They pitied her for the kidnapping and the long, terrible confinement, and felt guilty for not realizing that she and Tray needed rescue, or how to do it. They weren't sure whether to be happy for her and Tray, or feel loyal to Fask, as the jilted groom. And Fask, though he was unfailingly polite, was clearly disappointed by the outcome.

The Alaskan royalty probably resented that she hadn't turned out to be the neat solution to their question of succession. Quite the opposite, she had managed to confuse the issue even more and no one could agree who was technically the crown prince now. As oldest, it fell to Tray, but Toren had found his mate first. Rian seemed to think he had dodged a bullet by being in the middle by both age and chronology, but Tray and Toren were both swift to point out that he was the most *kingly* of all of them.

"Oh, lights," Tray said, taking her by the hand and leading her eagerly down a back hallway. "Is this as terrible for you as it is for me?" He had finally been able to shave, and his jaw was alluringly bare. It was hard for Leinani to keep her hands off of it when they were alone. She thought she'd loved the beard, but really she was just crazy about him in all of his smooth-to-scruffy permutations.

"It's weird that you can't tell," Leinani said with a wry chuckle. "It was so strange having you in my head, and now it's strange that you aren't there anymore."

Tray drew up before a doorway and put Leinani's hand on his chest. "I may not have you in my head now, but I will always, always have you in my heart," he said.

"That's poetic of you," Leinani said, smiling slowly, stepping closer. "And yes, it's kind of terrible facing everyone, but I'm so happy to be here with you now, that it's worth a little awkwardness. It will get easier."

"If any one of my brothers gives you any grief, I will personally knock them down," Tray promised.

"No one has given me any grief," Leinani promised. "Everyone has been extremely kind."

"Oh, no, not kind," Tray teased. "Anything but kind." His voice was light, but behind his joking, Leinani knew that he felt the same disconnect from reality that she did. It was so weird to be able to walk freely, to go through a doorway without flinching, to feel air at her neck where the choker had been for so long.

When she put her arms around him and leaned her head against his chest, he wrapped his arms around her and held tight. She wasn't sure which of them was comforting the other, but she drew strength from his embrace and tried to pour it back into him.

Quips aside, she knew that they would both have a lot to work through, and she was so glad that they would be able to do it together.

"Your surprise," Tray reminded her, after they'd soaked a measure of relief from each other. "You'll want a coat, we're going outside."

There was an arctic entrance with a rack of plain coats in

a range of sizes. Leinani took a blue parka that looked somewhat worse for the wear, slipped the banana into the pocket, and pulled the hood up over her head as Tray shrugged into a gray jacket and found a hat in a bin. There were mittens, and several pairs of boots. Leinani took the smallest. "What a remarkable selection of footwear," she teased. "I would have liked this many choices at our last accommodations."

"I never did get my hockey skates back," Tray complained, tossing her a pair of mittens.

"They would have been hard to escape in," Leinani pointed out.

He opened the outer door, and a whirl of icy air fogged the little chamber. There was bright daylight outside; it was nearly noon. Leinani's sense of time was badly confused, between the northern cycles of light and the time zones they'd traveled. Leinani was glad to find that although she could feel the biting cold on her cheeks, it didn't bother her. She gave her dragon the mental equivalent of a grateful hug.

I belong here, the creature replied contentedly.

"Where are we going?" Leinani wanted to know, as they traipsed along a shoveled path towards some outbuildings.

"I thought you'd enjoy a scenic tour of the property!" Tray said breezily.

"You did not," Leinani scolded him. "Where are you taking me?"

He gave her a smiling sideways look. "Therapy," he said. "You'll see."

They ended up at an outbuilding that Leinani thought might be a barn, and their approach did not go unannounced. There were straw-filled boxes in a loose grid, each with a lead and a bowl. Most of the spots were empty, but the closest ones had dogs, straining at the ends of their leads, barking and whining in joy. "The puppies are inside," Tray said, leading her in.

The building wasn't insulated, but it was considerably warmer than being outside in the elements. The floor was concrete, scattered with straw, and they were greeted with a chorus of yips and playful growls. There were four puppies, just as Tray had described, with legs like springs, and he had to nudge them back with his knee to get them safely into the building and latch the door behind them. Then he knelt down and was promptly swarmed. "You got so big!" he crowed at them.

One of them left off licking him and came to investigate Leinani, bouncing and putting front paws on her pants. "Oh," she said in surprise, bracing herself against his weight. "Aren't you darling!"

She crouched next to Tray and two of the other puppies switched targets to come and lick at her face and shove their noses into her sore side as they tried to climb her.

"Oh, oh!" Only dragon-sharp reflexes kept her upright under their assault.

They were feather-soft and as wiggly as advertised, squirming and whining in delight, and Leinani finally gave up trying to keep her balance and simply sat down, letting them love their way into her arms and investigate her hair with their snuffling noses. Tray had his remaining puppy over on its side, kicking legs in the air as he rubbed its furry belly.

"That one's Carina's Moose," he pointed out. "And that one's Tansy, Tania's pup. This is Lancelot, and you've got Milo in your lap."

"Hi, Milo," Leinani said, giggling helplessly. Milo

licked her face enthusiastically and snuggled close, his paws scratching on her parka.

Tray found a ball in the straw, whistled, and tossed it to the far side of the building. Milo pushed off of her with all four legs and raced with the others to fetch it.

They were back in a few moments, Moose triumphant with the ball, trying to keep it away from her siblings as she pranced just out of arm's length from Tray.

"I can't throw it for you if you don't give it to me," he scolded her, and she finally surrendered her slobbery prize.

All four dogs thundered across the floor, shoving shoulder-to-shoulder after the coveted ball. Fetching the ball seemed to disintegrate into wrestling and chewing on each other, and Milo snuck away from his siblings to grab the forgotten toy and return with it. He passed Tray and brought the ball to Leinani, growling playfully.

"I don't want that disgusting thing," she told him, reaching to stroke his head between his upright ears.

Milo nosed her insistently, whining, then dropped the ball in her lap. "Ew!" Leinani could not help but say, and she distastefully picked it up and tossed it into the straw. Milo pounced after it, attracting the attention of the other puppies, and there was an all-out tousle for it.

Tansy left the commotion to come sniff at Leinani, and got pets for her trouble. Then she sniffed Leinani, putting a nose in her armpit. She rather abruptly discovered the apple banana in the princess's pocket and her tail went mad. "You can't eat my banana," Leinani protested, pulling it away. This only made it a game, and all four puppies decided it was the new prize, attacking her with tongues and eager paws.

"Save my banana!" she cried to Tray, holding it aloft and toppling over backwards. She was laughing, and being licked, and puppy spit was somehow not as bad as she had expected it to be.

He saved them both, swooping in to lift her out of the sea of eager dogs and kiss her. "Will you share your banana if I save it?" he asked.

"Maybe I'll trade it for *your* banana," Leinani said suggestively.

"You have a deal," Tray said, eyes crinkling with laughter. "You want to go back to my room and play a game of Scrabble? Did you know that it actually has like four U's?"

"I won't know what to do with them!" Leinani giggled, and she kissed Tray, because it made her so happy that she could, any time she wanted now. "Yes, let's do that."

He put her back down on her feet and kicked the forgotten ball to distract the puppies away from them so they could slip out of the door.

"Best therapy?" Tray asked, as they wandered back towards the castle, arms around each other, squinting against the bright sunlight off of snow.

"Best therapy," Leinani agreed. "I like your puppies." She did feel better, just for being around only Tray, for petting the eager little creatures, for not having to act like everything was normal for a little while. The puppies didn't care if she'd been kidnapped, as long she gave them attention.

"I think Milo may adopt you," Tray warned.

"Doesn't pet adoption usually work the other way around?"

"How little you know dogs," Tray snorted. "I think that—"

Whatever he was going to say was lost as there was a sudden flare to the sparkle off the ice and a dragon landed in a puff of snow, folding dark wings back against its deep blue sides. In a flash, he was a man, a wild-bearded, dark-haired figure wearing a Native parka. "Where's Fask?" he roared, wading through the snowbank.

"Is that your brother Kenth?" Leinani guessed, while he was still out of earshot.

"Where's *Fask*?" Kenth repeated, clearly furious as he raged towards them.

"It's nice to see you, too, Kenth" Tray hollered in return. "He's inside, doing kingly stuff the rest of us don't want to do. What are you doing here?"

Kenth had made it to the shoveled pathway and he burst through in a shower of snow clumps. He didn't pause to make conversation, only stomped towards the castle and threw back over his shoulder, "My daughter is gone!"

Tray drew up short and Leinani clutched at her banana in alarm.

He was throwing open the back door that they'd come through before they could catch up with him, leaving it open behind him as he stormed in.

"Wait!" Tray called. "You have a daughter?! When did you have a daughter? No one ever tells me anything!"

∼

A NOTE FROM ELVA BIRCH

Thank you so much for picking up The Dragon Prince's Bride! I really loved writing this story and absolutely adore Tray and Leinani. I can't wait to write the next book - it's available for preorder now, and you can read on for a sneak preview!

Your reviews are very much appreciated; I read them all and they help other readers decide whether or not to buy my books!

A huge thank you to all of my fabulous beta readers and copy editors; any errors that remain are entirely my own. If you do find lingering typos—or you'd just like share your thoughts with me!—please feel free to email me at elvaherself@elvabirch.com. My cover was designed by Ellen Million.

To find out about my new releases, you can follow me on Amazon, subscribe to my newsletter, or like me on Facebook. Join my Reader's Retreat on Facebook for sneak previews and cut scenes! Find all the links at my webpage: elvabirch.com

I also write under other pen names—keep reading for information about my other available titles...

MORE BY ELVA BIRCH

A Day Care for Shifters: A hot new full-length series about adorable shifter kids and their struggling single parents in a town full of mystery and surprise. Start the series with Wolf's Instinct, when Addison comes to Nickel City to take a job at a very special day care and finds a family to belong to. A gentle ice-cream-straight-from-the-container escape. Sweet and sizzling!

∽

The Royal Dragons of Alaska: A fascinating alternate world where Alaska is ruled by secret dragon shifters. Adventure, romance, and humor! Reluctant royalty, relentless enemies…dogs, camping, and magic! Start with The Dragon Prince of Alaska.

∽

Suddenly Shifters: A hilarious series of novellas, serials, and shorts set in the small town of Anders Canyon, where something (in the water?) is making ordinary citizens turn into shifters. Start with Something in the Water! Also available in audio!

∽

Birch Hearts: An enchanting collection of short stories and novellas. Unconstrained by theme or setting, each short read has romance, magic, and heart, with a satisfying conclusion. And always, the impossible and irresistible. Start with a sampler plate in Prompted 2 for fourteen pieces of sweet-to-sizzling flash fiction, or dive in with the novella, Better Half. Breakup is a free story!

WRITING AS ZOE CHANT

Shifting Sands Resort: A complete ten-book series - plus two collections of shorts. This is a thrilling shifter romance set at a tropical island resort. Each book stands alone but connects into a great mystery with a thrilling conclusion. Start with Tropical Tiger Spy or dive in to the Omnibus edition, with all of the novels, short stories, and novellas in my preferred reading order!

∽

Fae Shifter Knights: A complete four-book fantasy portal romp, with cute pets and swoon-worthy knights stuck in a world of wonders like refrigerators and ham sandwiches. Start with Dragon of Glass!

∽

Green Valley Shifters: A sweet, small town series with single dads, secret shifters, sweet kids, and spinsters. Low-peril and steamy! Standalone books where you can revisit your favorite characters - this series is also complete! Start with Dancing Barefoot!

Also by Zoe Chant (but not Elva Birch): **Virtue Shifters**: Sexy and funny, each book set in the little town of Virtue promises a heartwarming story, a touch of fate, and a little bit of adventure. Start with Timber Wolf!

THE BOOK I'M NOT WRITING

Writing as Elva Birch
She's got one life to live

Anita takes a chance at a job she's not sure she can handle and she's tickled pink when the gorgeous billionaire picks her little bakery to cater his big charity event. But what was supposed to be the opportunity of a lifetime turns into the storm of a century.

He's got one leg to stand on

Frank Wilson has built his reputation and his world-spanning lawn ornament business on one tenet: honesty. There's nothing fake about Frank Wilson -- not his fabulous fortune or his amazing physique.

...or his inner flamingo.

Trapped together with his fated mate in his big empty office building with two thousand gourmet cupcakes and no power, Frank is sure that -- finally -- nothing will stand between him and everything that he'd ever wanted, in the arms of a curvy woman wearing an apron. The only problem is, she's not interested in settling down to join his flock.

And to win her heart, he's going to have to put his foot down.

∼

I love to do harmless April Fool's Day pranks, and I made this cover for my readers, even going so far as to make a book blurb and fake Amazon book preview image for Facebook.

But the joke's on me and this, of all of the books I have planned, is the one I have the most readers clamoring for!

I am not writing it. I am not writing the scene where Anita plays Simon Says and makes Frank stand on one foot forever. I am not plotting the chapter where they are dancing around the empty ballroom. I am not researching all the flamingo jokes on the internet.

If you would like to read more of the book I'm very definitely not writing, you'll have to sign up for my mailing list at elvabirch.com or join Elva Birch's Readers Retreat at Facebook!

CHAPTER 1 OF THE DRAGON PRINCE'S SECRET

Mackenzie felt alone in the sea of strangers at the lavish late breakfast table.

They were all quite kind, offering her decadent seconds of amazing food and kindly overlooking the times that she fumbled some attempt at manners that she only knew from books.

But if the severe woman in a guard's uniform sitting at the end of the table looked particularly suspicious, it was understandable. Mackenzie had, up until just the day before, been working for a cult known as The Cause run by a woman named Amara who had tried to steal the Alaskan's magical artifacts, kidnapped Prince Tray and Princess Leinani, and used magic to temporarily strip the them of their dragons.

Mackenzie had helped the two escape, but no one really trusted a turncoat, did they?

She tugged her shirtsleeve down at her wrist, even there was no real chance of the tattoo on her forearm showing. The axe in a simplified labyrinth was the symbol of the Cause, an indelible mark of her upbringing as their enemy.

When Tray and Leinani snuck out of the meal, followed shortly after by Leinani's nearly-hysterical mother and consoling father, Mackenzie felt more bereft than ever. She didn't know anyone else in the room and she didn't know how to broach the topic closest to her heart.

Her purpose in freeing the dragon royalty had been to secure allies who could help her free Amara's other captives, but since the rescue late the night before, she had been unable to present her case. The kind older woman whose care she had been entrusted to had brushed off her tentative attempts at asking for access to an authority and instead had insisted that Mackenzie rest and have her wounds treated. Mackenzie didn't know how to explain the urgency of her real mission here without being rude. She tried to be patient and navigate all the customs and culture that she didn't understand.

Should she make an official appeal to Prince Fask, as the eldest brother? Or did that entreaty go to Prince Toren, the youngest of the brothers, but the first with a formal mate according to the Compact that governed them?

She had expected to be brought for questioning that morning, not served a decadent feast. She couldn't figure out the chain of command from their friendly joking. Though she was introduced to each of them in turn, even that seemed to be in order of convenience rather than influence.

She cataloged them in her head. Toren's mate was Carina. Also an American, Tania was the staid woman beside her with a cane over the arm of her chair and the quiet, bookish prince beside her was Rian, one of the middle brothers. Prince Raval largely ignored the conversation but gave a distant nod of acknowledgment when Mackenzie was introduced around like an honored guest. Drayger, alarmingly, winked at her when he was presented, and clarified that he was a bastard of the Majorca royal dragons.

The conversation ebbed and flowed around her, and while they generously included her in praise for the meal, observations about the weather, and general gossip about royals that Mackenzie knew vaguely by name, she had little to contribute.

Her side hurt, and she was plagued by her purpose.

Finally, as the breakfast vanished and the dishes were cleared away, the discussion came back around to more serious topics.

Fask eyed them all, and Mackenzie thought that he looked as suspicious of Drayger as he did of herself. "I want you all to keep to the castle for a time," he said frankly. "With the new year, there has been a great deal of political unrest and we're doing damage control. There have been riots and independent media has been spinning us in a very...unfavorable light."

"Here in Fairbanks?" Raval said in astonishment. "The worst we tend to get are people protesting the potholes like we're personally responsible for frost heaves."

"The Cause has been busy," Fask said. Then his gaze did fall on Mackenzie. "They've stepped up their rhetoric and there are private reports of several assassination attempts over the new year. We weren't worried about the protests in the past, but these seem to be more organized, more driven, more heavily armed. People are getting hurt."

Mackenzie felt her heart race and the rich meal was

heavy in her stomach. Here came the interrogation she'd been expecting.

Fask's voice wasn't exactly unkind, but it wasn't terribly warm, either. "What can you tell us about the Cause, Mackenzie?"

Mackenzie drew a breath, prepared for the question. "The Cause has been around, more quietly, for many years. Amara was a charismatic leader and she gathered a cult of followers who disbelieved the cover story of the Small Kingdoms. She was convinced there was a great conspiracy of magic and corruption. For a long time, she preached a path of rejecting magic and the supernatural as impure and evil.

"But her story took a sudden turn as she realized what magic could do for her, and she has changed her creed from the certainty that magic should be purged to the idea that she should control all of it herself. Our—their—purpose shifted from destroying magic to stealing it."

"You can't make a change that drastic to an entire religion, can you?" Toren sounded pretty uncertain for a prince.

Did they disbelieve her?

"You can if you control all of the media for a select group of people." Rian was a more thoughtful-looking mirror image of his twin brother. "Tray said you worked directly for Amara."

"Yes," Mackenzie said without pride. "I was...her hand."

"What did you do for her?"

Their curiosity was as logical as their suspicions. "I read magic. If I can see the spell, I can tell what it does."

"You mean, you're good at guessing what it does from what is written." Rian had that pushy curiosity that

Mackenzie associated with librarians. She trusted him instinctively because she trusted librarians.

"No," Mackenzie said quietly but firmly. "I don't guess. When I see a spell, I know what it will do. I know the words of power, the limitations, and deflections, even if they aren't written out explicitly. It is my gift." Amara had always called it a gift. Mackenzie had come to regard it as a curse, a terrible burden that made her useful to all the wrong people. Maybe, for once, she could be useful to the right people.

At her words, all of their heads swiveled towards one of the princes. Raval, Mackenzie remembered. One of the middle brothers, the one who was a caster himself.

"Is that possible?" Rian wanted to know.

Raval shrugged. "It's nothing I've ever heard of, but that doesn't mean it isn't *possible.*"

"Can we test this?" the woman next to him asked. Tania, Mackenzie remembered from the wave of introductions. She was Rian's mate and she had an ornate cane leaning beside her chair. "Maybe show her one of your spells?"

Raval looked outraged, as if he had just been asked to undress in public.

"I am happy to submit to your tests," Mackenzie said fervently. They had to believe her. If they didn't trust her, they wouldn't help her. If they wouldn't help her...she didn't know what else she could do, and she wasn't willing to admit defeat.

"We could show her the Compact," Toren said lightly.

"She's not to be admitted to the vault," Fask snapped. He looked alarmed at the idea, and no wonder; Amara had tried twice now to steal the Compact. "We will test your claim, but I'm sure that you are still weary from your ordeal and injury."

Mackenzie resisted touching the place at her side that still felt hot. It hurt less now, just a dull ache, but if she slouched in her chair, it sometimes surprised her with a jolt of pain.

She opened her mouth to thank him for the thoughtfulness and protest that she wanted to help and that there wasn't any time to waste, because—

The door to the dining hall burst open and a furious figure barged in, shedding snow. Tray and Leinani were right behind him, still dressed for the outdoors.

"Fask! Fask, you bastard, *where is she?*"

A quick glance around showed that everyone else was just as surprised as Mackenzie was, but none of them looked particularly afraid; this wasn't a stranger to all of the brothers, at least. There were guards outside the dining hall that sheepishly closed the door behind him.

The intruder was wild-looking, with long hair and a scruffy beard. He was dressed in a worn Native parka and his hands were in mittens. Mackenzie suspected by his posture that they were balled in fists, and Toren was rising to his feet. "Kenth?"

This was the brother she hadn't met, the second oldest. He looked like he'd just wandered straight in from months in the wilderness. He didn't pay any of them the slightest mind, striding directly to Fask and menacing over him. "Where is she?!"

Fask looked as shocked as any of them and he stood. "What are you talking about, Kenth?"

"No one else knew about her, Fask. She was stolen out of her bed this morning, through a portal, and no one else knew about her!"

Fask had a politician's voice. Mackenzie knew too well those measured tones, that careful way of speaking. Amara spoke like that, and it set the hairs on the back of her neck to attention.

"Kenth," he said, "I have no idea what you're talking about. Calm down and tell us what's happening."

"Dalaya!" Kenth roared. "Someone kidnapped Dalaya!"

"Who is Dalaya?" Toren wanted to know.

"Dalaya is my daughter!"

That made a murmur of shock and speculation swirl around the table and Mackenzie watched in fascination as the people accepted this revelation with a range of reactions. Carina looked delighted. Toren looked dazed. Raval's brow was furrowed in confusion and Tania and Rian were exchanging skeptical looks.

"You have a daughter?"

"Since when?"

"Congratulations?"

"What the hell?!"

A secret child? At least Mackenzie wasn't the only one who seemed to have no clue what was happening.

"Calm down, Kenth. Of course, we'll use all of our resources to find her," Fask promised, rising to his feet. "Captain Luke will get a team on it. A discreet team."

Kenth had not given Fask a breath of room as he stood and was still snarling into his face. "Who did you tell?"

Fask met his angry gaze with impressive serenity. "I know we've had our differences," he said firmly, "but I wouldn't harm a child, and I've kept your secret."

"Who would take her? Why would they want her?" Kenth looked like he might like to wring the answers from Fask's broken body, like he was on the brink of unleashing his fury on his brother, held back by his own bared teeth. Several of the brothers had gotten to their feet now, and were ranged around the two like they were ready to haul them off of each other at any moment.

"Who kidnaps children?" Toren asked, horrified.

"Ransom?" That was Toren's wife, Carina. "People do dastardly things for money."

Amara. Amara kidnapped children. Children were easy to control, and their flexible young minds meant that they were susceptible to some of Amara's favorite tricks. Mackenzie stared at her plate, not sure how to volunteer the information, then lifted her chin. "Is she a caster?"

"What?" Raval, across the table, was the only one who had heard her.

"The child. Is she...is she a natural caster?"

All of the attention in the room was suddenly focused overwhelmingly upon Mackenzie.

"Amara...talked about getting a great prize at the new year." Had that only been last night? Time zones confused her sense of passing time.

She looked up to find that Kenth was staring down the table at her, confusion and amazement on his face.

"Who are you?" he asked in wonder. He seemed to have forgotten entirely about Fask.

"This is Mackenzie," Toren said. "She was recently rescued from a cult that kidnapped Tray and Princess Leinani of Mo'orea." He gestured to where Tray and Leinani were standing together in the doorway, still dressed in parkas and boots. "Mackenzie helped them escape."

"Leinani?" Kenth appeared to have been stupefied, and he was still gazing down the table at Mackenzie, who was beginning to feel seriously unnerved by his regard.

"Leinani was supposed to be Fask's bride," Carina explained. "She's Tray's mate, instead."

"You've missed a lot," Rian said wryly. "Most of it in the last few months."

Kenth paid them no mind whatsoever as he pushed past Toren to stride down the table to Mackenzie, who sat frozen in her chair because she didn't know what else to do.

"Who *are* you?" he repeated.

Mackenzie looked up into his face, wondering if she had done something wrong. He was handsome, behind the scruffy beard and the stormy anger in his face, and his eyes were bright silver.

Before she could answer, he was hastily saying, "No, don't be afraid, don't ever be afraid of me. You're hurt!"

She was so tense that the wound in her side was burning again, fiery, and her breath was shallow in her lungs.

To her astonishment, Kenth dropped into the empty chair next to her like his knees had failed him.

"M-Mackenzie," she told him, though Toren had already introduced her, and she got the feeling that her name was not what he was looking for.

"Mackenzie," he repeated in wonder. "And you are *my* mate."

"I'm sorry, what?" Mackenzie was keenly aware that they were the focus of every pair of eyes in the room. Even the iron-faced guard, Captain Luke, looked like she was holding her breath.

"*Another* one?" Toren said quietly after a moment.

"Don't you feel it?" Kenth asked gently.

Mackenzie wondered if this was some kind of elaborate test, a method of initiation. "Feel...what?"

Silence answered her, then Tania, Rian's mate, offered kindly, "It's a little confusing, I know. It's like you can feel everything he can, all of the emotions you have now, and those that you will have after you have fallen in love."

"It's the magic of the Compact," Rian said from beside

Tania, covering her hand with his own. "It helps the heir to the kingdom to find their mate and lets them know each other when they meet."

Mackenzie knew about the Compact, of course. It was, officially, a treaty that bound all of the Small Kingdoms in matters of trade and defense and succession. She'd always assumed that the *mate* that it referenced was nothing more than a fanciful title for the diplomatic marriage alliances that powerful countries made to ensure their security.

But she also knew that the true nature of the Compact was magic. Amara coveted control of the document with a passion that bordered on obsession, sure that it was the key to controlling all of the magic in the world, and she often spoke of the power she would have when she owned it.

Mackenzie looked around the table. Did they mean to imply that the mates were actually magic love connections, chosen by the enchanted document?

It certainly sounded poetic, and clearly they all believed in it, but Mackenzie felt nothing from this rather alarming and intense stranger facing her.

"I'm...I'm sorry," she said quietly. "It's part of my gift. Magic doesn't work on me."

∼

Get The Dragon Prince's Secret now!

Printed in Dunstable, United Kingdom